BARRON

A CROSS TO BEAR Book 5

KATHI S. BARTON

This is a work of fiction. Names, characters, places, and incidents are products of the author's imagination or are used fictitiously and are not to be construed as real. Any resemblance to actual events, locations, organizations, or persons, living or dead, is entirely coincidental.

World Castle Publishing, LLC
Pensacola, Florida

Copyright © 2024 Kathi S. Barton
Paperback ISBN: 9798891261822
eBook ISBN: 9798891261839
First Edition World Castle Publishing, LLC, March 25, 2024
http://www.worldcastlepublishing.com

Licensing Notes

Cover: Karen Fuller
Editor: Karen Fuller

Chapter 1

Caitlynn filed the paperwork in the file and put it behind her on the credenza with the rest of the work she'd been catching up on. Looking up, she was startled to see that Barron was sitting across from her. Smiling, she asked him if he'd gotten things squared away already.

"I did. For the most part, anyway. I have an order in for goats and pigs to be delivered to the farm in a few days after we return." She corrected him, saying if they returned. "They'll come by rail car and then be delivered to the farm in semi-trucks. I'm about as excited to have them as I am to have new stock coming in. This way, I can play around with the different kinds of goat milk that I'll get from them." She asked him if it was a huge difference, letting him ignore the fact that they had talked about returning or not. "I don't know if it'll be huge, but it will be different than just the Boer goats that I have now. And you don't really care."

"I do. I promise you. I was just thinking about the fact that you're excited about goats like I am about advertising a new product. It suits you to be this happy. Everything about us being here seems to make you happy. Don't you think?" He thanked her. "Did you have any luck finding yourself some sheep? I know that was on your list while we were here in town."

She and Barron had started talking to each other three weeks ago. A very long phone conversation that had them both knowing, just by that, that they were meant to be together. He told her how she was his partner, his friend, and she couldn't have been happier if he'd asked her right then to marry him. Caitlynn knew that if he ever did, she wouldn't hesitate to say yes. He meant that much to her.

She'd spoken to him on the phone when one of her ex-employees had come to talk to him. Really, he'd been manhandling him about letting her company buy his cheese and sausages company

that he made to sell in their local shop. Since he'd
made it very clear to Denver Longshot that he had
no desire to sell his company, she'd never once
asked him — for that matter, thought about asking
him to allow her to buy him out. Caitlynn could
and would have if he wanted, but she thought
that it wouldn't be as good as the good hometown
charm that he put into everything that he made.
So long as he could figure out how to put it in it
without actually being there.

Every time he spoke of the goats and his
other animals, she could see how much passion he
had for them. His love for them and the things that
they gave him were something special. And his
joy in making what he did with their product was
something so refreshing that she couldn't help but
be excited when he was. Also? Well, she could wait
for that passion to lessen, and then he'd be all hers.
The milkers — his cows and lambs, he had named
each and every one of them as soon as they were
purchased or born on the mountain. She really
enjoyed his mannerisms of being a compassionate
man and a good man to be around.

"Several of the farmers said that sheep are
just curly goats. I'm not sure that's right, but I

did find out that I'd be better off with llamas than sheep. They need a great deal of room to roam, and while I have that, he also said that they can be slightly aggressive toward other animals. The fencing needs to be better than I have already for the cows. Which is going to be work. I'm thinking keeping the bears out with them will be a big chore when they smell them." He got him a cup of water from the water dispenser. Never bottled, she noticed. Maybe he didn't care for the plastic taste. When he was finished with his drink, he tossed the paper cup into the recycling bin marked paper.

"I'm still weighing my opinion on them, to be honest. I don't know if he was trying to make sure that I didn't buy them from his neighbor and the llamas from him or if he was telling the truth. I should have done more research on them. But I do have a good idea about the wool I would get from them." She knew that he did. Barron had told her from the start that he wanted to branch out a little more, that he thought that making throw rugs to go with his wine and cheese set would be the perfect thing for a young couple to have. He even told her that they'd have to try them out when the weather got warmer. "Are you about ready to go?

Or do you have more work to do? I can come back. I have a couple of meetings in the morning that I can get some information on from the computer."

"No, I'm ready." Closing up her filing cabinet, she was so thrilled when he came up behind her and nibbled on her neck. They'd not had sex yet, she couldn't wait, but she knew that they'd come pretty close a few times. "Are we having dinner with that guy again tonight?"

"No." She liked that answer and told him so. "I had my sisters do some looking into his life. He's not nearly as clean-cut as he makes out to be. Also, you might want to rethink hiring Mr. Darby. Jamie said that she'd speak to you later about him. However, we are having dinner with a friend of mine. I hope you don't mind."

"So long as at the end of the dinner, we go home together." He kissed her neck and then turned her around in his arms. "Barron, are you ever going to fuck me?" He laughed. Hard too.

"Baby, you have no idea how much I want to right now. But, as I told you before, you're ovulating, and we don't want to have children right away. You're still thinking that, correct?" She nodded, then shook her head. "Yeah, I'm right there with you. By the way, Rusty and Joey got their packages today. So did the kids. Thad, he's my favorite little man. He told me that he's going to make his first project for you. Since I don't know what that might be, I'm sure that it will be amazing."

It made her smile every time that they talked. There was no subject too taboo for them to talk about. Even if it was sex, they would talk about their likes and dislikes when it came to making love. Neither of them seemed to be in too much of a hurry to make love, especially Barron. Also, about their businesses. He would and had come to her with questions about sales, and she came to him about different projects that she was thinking of purchasing to sell, too.

Most of the time, they talked about the mountain and how much he wished he could have all the things that the big city offered him, as well as the country life that he'd grown up with on the mountain. But every time, he would say that the mountain was where his heart was, and she believed him.

They were seated right away when they arrived at the restaurant. Barron, for all his country boy charm, was a very sophisticated man. He knew wines, of course, and topics about everything, including politics. He could talk about farming as well as a spreadsheet that he'd come up with to keep track of sales. There weren't too many subjects that he didn't have some knowledge of. But what she liked most about him was that he had no trouble at all telling her that he didn't know something when she'd ask him about it.

"Okay, you might be surprised to see who we're having dinner with. I know that when I was called this morning to set this up, I was surprised, too." He smiled at her as he looked over his shoulder. "I didn't think that he'd be incognito, however. Or so he thinks he is. I knew him as soon as I saw him. Honey, just act like you're old friends."

She put out her cheek to be kissed when the man who joined them leaned into her. She had to cover her laughter when she realized that the man, whoever he was, really was dressed up—

"You're the president." He nodded, then smiled at her. The ugly wig came off, and he nodded to someone who was still behind her. She looked at Barron. "I had no idea…Well, I should have known that you'd have connections with people who are high on the food chain. Should I still act like I know you, sir?"

"You can if you want, but I'd rather get to know you like this, in a nice restaurant. Everyone here is on my payroll, so it's a moot point to pretend that no one knows who I am. Barron and I go way back. I think it was kindergarten. Right?" Barron said it was preschool. "That's right. I remember now. We were in different rows in class but right across from each other. He saved my nerdy life a few times in high school, too."

"You always say that to people. But all I did was point out to the bully that you were too skinny and nerdy to beat the crap out of when there were bigger targets around that he could mess with." Roger said, laughing that Barron had pointed out his older brother. "Yeah, I did. The kid was never a bully again after that. His name was Aaron Spike if I remember correctly. The last time I saw him, he was running for mayor of our town. I think he was run out, much like my brother did to him when he decided to pick on someone much bigger than him. Aaron wasn't a good person to anyone. How are you, Roger?"

"Your family, they know that you eat dinner with the president?" Barron told her that it had never come up. "So I'm the...you know, this is great. I know that I can't tell anyone, but it's very good to meet you, sir. So what's this meeting about? I have places to be later if you need me out of the way."

Roger laughed. Very hard, too, and Caitlynn knew that he'd not done that in a long time. He'd seemed as surprised as she was when he did it. After a plate of appetizers was set before them, she took off the first thing that she wanted and put them on her plate. The deep-fried raviolo was her favorite snack of all time.

"Greedy, aren't you. It's a good thing that I have ordered extra to be brought out in a few minutes. As for you leaving, never when I'm around, young lady. If I want to talk about something, I'll find Barron later." She told him her name. "I know you're more than likely aware that I've done a thorough background check on you and found you to be delightfully without skeletons in your closet. There are a couple way back in your line, but nothing that anyone would care all that much for now. I'm here to talk to Barron about a project that he came to me with several years ago. The prison farms."

"You said it would cost too much." Roger said it still would, but it would work out better because he had an idea. "All right. And if you need numbers, you know that I have them. What sort of prison farms are you thinking about? The ones that I came to you with or the ones I sent to you later. I think that one would—"

"Stop talking in riddles, please? What farms are we working on?" Caitlynn smiled at them when she realized that she'd been snippy to them both. Roger told her three that Barron had come up with. She just stared at him. "Prisoners farming for their own food? I think that's a brilliant idea. I don't know a great deal about cattle yet, but I do know that pound for pound, they have a good pay off. Not like fruits and vegetables, but...I like this idea a great deal."

"There are issues with it, however. And I have to admit that when he broached me with the idea, I turned him down flat. The prison system is so overloaded now, it would be hard to keep track of all of the men and women while working in the grounds." Barron started to speak, but Roger stopped him. "I went back and reread the proposal and found that you put in there that only the good guys were able to work outdoors. You're not going to believe this, but Barron also said that the hardest criminals should have the option of working in the gardens for their one hour a day outside. I honestly think that's the best idea of all. It's not like I wouldn't have enough guards around them at all times."

"You wouldn't just make it mandatory, would you?" Roger asked her why she'd think it shouldn't be. "Then they won't enjoy it. I can understand why some people wouldn't want to be put out in a garden, made to work for their food. But if you give them the option to say, I don't know, they sort of reap what they grow with getting a little extra in their plates. Or once a week. I would have to give that some thought. But maybe you might have more workers than you need. However, the overall products coming into the kitchen, the healthy aspect, it shouldn't come up. I can't imagine too many inmates would be all that thrilled about eating healthy when they know that they're never going to get out of the four walls that they're behind."

"Roger has actually thrown around the idea of selling the products. Including the beef or whatever they decided to have on the farms. It would help with a few of the inmates that don't have anyone filling their commissary funds for them." She started to shake her head and then said she didn't know about that. "I can see a couple of reasons for not selling it, but you tell me what you think."

"Greed." She looked at Roger. "I'm not saying that you'd be like this, but my thoughts keep coming back to that movie with Morgan Freeman and Tim Robbins. The prison one they were in. Remember that? How the warden of the prison... what was his name? Anyway, he was taking bribes centered around the work they were doing from business owners that couldn't underbid—Bob Gunton, that's him. I just saw that movie about a month ago. The only people who were benefiting from the roads being done by the prisoners were the man in charge of them. I know you are a good person, or Barron would have killed you decades ago, but what about the new warden or the next one? That could cause an uprising that would get a lot of people killed."

The president stood up and put his hands on either side of her face, and kissed her. After sitting back down, he laughed. And continued laughing for so long that she wanted to smack him. Temptation was great, but there was also a room full of secret service there too.

"I don't know what I should be more thankful for. The fact that you don't think that I'm a greedy bastard or that all those after me would be. Thank you, my darling. I'll have to tell my wife. Just this morning, she called me that very thing when I took all the covers from her side of the bed." He laughed a bit more, then he moaned when his dinner was sat in front of him. "I do love a good piece of salmon grilled to perfection."

They didn't talk much after their dinners were served. She'd gotten the salmon as well and thought it the best she'd ever tasted. Barron, however, was having a thick porterhouse steak. No potato, no veggies of any kind, but a side bowl of mushroom gravy that he dipped his bite-sized pieces of steak in as he devoured it. He even offered her a bit of his so that she could know what she was missing. She wasn't much of a beef eater but did enjoy his.

After dinner, their plates were taken away, and they were offered coffee and tea. She wasn't a huge fan of coffee but did enjoy the smell of it. Roger had a glass of wine with his scones, and Barron had some tea. That, she had noticed, was the go-to drink for his entire family. Tea, hot or cold, so long as it wasn't sweetened.

The men talked a bit more about the project that Roger wanted Barron to oversee. She didn't have much to input but they did pull her in on occasion to ask her what she thought. When her cell phone rang, she got up and went to the bar with two of the men with the president to take it. It didn't bother her to have company, but it was a little odd.

"I was wondering if you have time for a meeting in the morning with me." She hadn't any idea who it was so she asked. There was no shame in asking, she thought. "Now, why should that matter until you tell me if you can meet with me or not?"

"Either tell me who this is, or I'll simply hang up. I'm not into games, nor do I work with people who think that they're funny when I'm trying to run a business." The serviceman with her asked her to put it on speaker. Handing it to him when she fumbled around with it, he stuck a device at the end of it and nodded for her to take it. "Are you there?"

"Yes. I'm working through my anger at you. You don't want to see me angry, Caitlynn. A great deal is riding on you cooperating with me." Suddenly, three men were surrounding her, all of them with their backs to her and their guns out. "Now, I'm going to ask you this again, politely, and you're going to either tell me—"

"No. I don't have time to have a meeting with you. Even if I had the whole day free, I'd not spend five minutes with you." When she started to hang up, the serviceman who had fixed her phone shook his head. But she didn't speak to the man on the other end but listened.

"I can hear you breathing, Caitlynn Royce. It's a sweet-sweet sound. One that you'd better appreciate before I catch up with you. Tell that boyfriend of yours that I'm coming for you, and once I find you...Well, I'm afraid there won't be much of you left. You'll understand when we meet that I'm a person who gets what he wants when he wants it. There will be no way for you to get away until I'm finished with you. Be forewarned, my dear Caitlynn, that you'll be begging me to allow you to be set free when the time comes." She huffed. Not meaning to do it aloud but he heard her all the same. "You think that I can't get to you? Well, let me show you how easy it is by hurting that boyfriend of yours."

The long case of liquor shattered in front of her, and the young man who'd been helping her with the phone dropped to the floor. She didn't have to look to know that he was dead. Blood and she hoped that was all it was sprayed all over her face when he was shot. Caitlynn started to scream. She opened her mouth and let go of all her fear when she was suddenly pressed against someone. As soon as she inhaled, she knew that it was Barron.

~*~

Listening to the conversation going on around him, Barron was trying his best to hold tightly onto his temper. He knew that whatever had happened had been beyond his control, that the man who had called her seemed to be harmless right up until he wasn't. Killing a federal agent was going to get every agency in the United States after him. But for now, he was going to worry about Caitlynn and only her.

"He thought that he was you." Barron asked her what she meant. "He said he was going to kill my boyfriend. He thought...oh that poor agent. He didn't deserve that. But the man talking, he thought that he was you. My boyfriend. He— Barron, I'm so afraid I can't make my own sense."

"I understand Caitlynne. The man on the phone thought he was killing me. He didn't understand nor know that you weren't alone and with agents." She nodded and laid her head back on his chest. "They rushed Roger home. They didn't want him to be photographed here with us. I can understand that, but I still worry about him."

"I'm ready to talk to the agents now. Though most of them were with me when...am I supposed to say that? I'm betting not."

"No. You just need to say that you were having dinner, and your phone rang. Stopping to answer it on your way to the ladies' room, and that's all you know. The man, you don't know who he was either. They want us to act like, not that it won't be hard to act like we were having a good dinner, then this man called. They're saying that the man who was killed was out with his wife, too, when he was suddenly in the wrong place at the wrong time. Christ, I should have gotten up with you. You've no idea how sorry I am that I didn't."

"You'd be dead if you had. I mean, I hate that the other man is dead, I truly am, but I'm glad that it wasn't you." She hugged him tightly, and he did the same to her.

Barron had forgotten that they needed to talk. Actually, he'd been putting things off. Important things that he should have spoken about when they were first together. He wasn't sure why he'd not told her of their immortality or any magic that they had now that they'd found one another. He knew that they got along very well and had been having fun, but there was something he didn't know what that was holding him back.

Barron also knew, too, that she wasn't ovulating. Most of the women he knew only had an ovulation period of sixteen to twenty-four hours. He just—he did want sex, but not with her. There was something there, something that he just couldn't put his finger on about her. That's when he realized that something was holding him back from telling her that he liked her. Liked...not loved but liked. He'd been meaning to reach out to one of his mated brothers to ask them what they thought of his thoughts on Caitlynn.

He'd been overwhelmed with grief. Not just that his grandparents had died a couple of weeks before hand, but he'd had one of his goats and her stillborn baby die that morning. It was simply too much for his heart to take that morning, and now here he was stuck…okay, he thought, he was stuck with Caitlynn.

It was nearly three in the morning when he was dropped off at his hotel. He'd been staying there since they arrived in Texas and enjoyed the fact that he could come and go when he needed to. Since he was usually up several hours before Caitlynn, he knew that he would disturb her when he left. She, of course, lived in her apartment.

There was enough about apartment living that he didn't care for, and that made him stick with his rooms at the hotel. It wasn't convenient, there were cars and buses to take him about, but it was quieter than her apartment. It felt to him like he could hear every pin drop that happened below and above them. And the best part was, he had his own big bed.

After closing down his computer and

looking over the sales that he'd made yesterday and the day before, he realized that it was nearly seven in the morning and reached out to his older brother, Mark. He'd tease him a bit, but once he asked him a few questions about mates, he knew that he'd get the best answers from him. After asking about Jamie, he told him what he'd been thinking about.

"*So you're saying that you don't have this overwhelming desire to mark her? Nor does your bear? That's not right, Barron. I'm sure you've figured that out on your own.*" Barron told him that he really didn't know if it was because she was his friend first. "*No. I don't think that's right. Claiming her, that would be a priority for you and your other half. You said you don't even care if you get to hang out with her. That should have been a big sign for you.*"

"*Not really. I've been around you guys when you found your mates. Each one of you had a different approach. Especially you. I mean, let's be honest, you were a real bastard to Jamie from the first. Then the others, they were sappy when they fell in love. Maybe I'm a late bloomer or something.*" Mark asked him if he really thought that. "*I don't know. I feel like... please don't say anything to anyone, Mark, but I feel like I could take her or leave her. I love hanging around with her. Sometimes. Talking to her about business is nice, but that's about it. I don't mind holding her hand, but I don't care if I do or not. Sometimes, especially here lately, I find that I want to just jerk my hand from hers and get ahead of her a little bit. You know, now that I say that out loud, it doesn't sound good, does it?"*

"No, it doesn't." Then he told him how he'd not told her about the magic. *"Does she have any? And another thing, do you have more? The one that you can tell for sure is when you shift, are you dressed in your same clothing?"*

"I've not had a reason to shift while I'm here." He said he was going to try it now. He did. Carefully shifting to his bear, then back to himself. It was actually a relief to him when he contacted his brother again. *"Mark, I'm naked. And I'm happy about it. That's really…what do you suppose is going on? Why did, at first, I feel like she was the one for me, but now, all I can think about is how much I want to get away from her clinging to me."*

He then told his brother about what had happened at the restaurant. Mark was sort of pissed that he'd not started with that conversation, but he told him that he wasn't hurt but did have a great deal on his mind. Mark said that he understood, but he should have told them when it happened.

"I suppose so. But this thing with Caitlynn is driving me nuts, like this morning. I just wanted to pack up my shit and come home. But…I have no desire to take her with me. I should, I really should, if for no other reason than to keep her safe. This other person, he doesn't know who I am or what I look like, so I'm not in any kind of hurry…Mark, I'm not in love with her. Nor do I believe that she's my mate. What do I do? Please tell me."

"Honestly? I haven't any idea. As much as I hate to mention this to you, because you know they're going to find out sooner rather than later is to talk to the women. I don't know why, but you know how they can get to the bottom of something quicker than anyone, and that's what you need. Answers. Before it's too late. And if you keep hanging out with her, she might well make it so that it's too late for you and her to separate." Barron asked him what he thought they'd do to him. "This is something that I've never heard of before. So I don't know how to judge what they're going to say. I will tell Jamie for you and see her reaction. That'll give you a heads up on what the others might do to you."

"I don't need to be knocked around. I'm feeling

damaged enough if you want to know the truth." He told him he was sorry and would tell her that, too. *"No. Christ, if you tell her that, she's going to knock me around for being a pussy. That is not something that I want."*

They were both laughing by the time he closed the connection between them. He knew that of all his brothers, Mark would be the most helpful and compassion. However, he'd never known the wives of his other brothers to beat around the bush about anything. It was then that he heard from Jamie.

"What do you know about wholesale markets?" He told her that he'd only been to a few of them, but they were mostly animals. *"Okay. Good. They'd have to be about the same, don't you think? I mean, products to buy and then to resell them, correct? I mean, you'd have to know what sort of pricing you could do with them according to your location and sales. Right?"*

"Yes. But remember, I'm not reselling my animals but using them for products. I wouldn't know the first thing about reselling merchandise. I have always left the pricing of my things by what Grannie told me to put on them. I would have been nearly giving my things away had it not for her doubling the price that I

had on the stuff in the first place. *I'm assuming you're meaning the shop."* She told him that she was going to purchase two buildings closer to the middle of town where she could put products. One of them being a shop that carried things made by the local Indian tribes. *"We did that once before. It didn't go over well, but I think it had more to do with the location than anything. If you have places closer to the heart of things, you might do a bit better than grannie did. In fact, I think there is a record book that she kept in her office at Grannie's place for every shop that she had. Maddy might have even found it already."*

"I'll ask her. Okay, I'll have to get back to you. Mark is wanting to talk to me." He told her that it was about him and to please be gentle. *"What's wrong? Never mind. I'll talk to Mark. Honey, you know that I love you, don't you?"*

"And I love you too, Jamie. More than words could be put to a poem." She told him that he was going to press her emotional buttons but closed the connection before he could speak to her.

It wasn't long before Jamie and the other woman popped into his room. He was glad that he'd pulled on his pants when he had, or they might be getting more than they dreamed about their little brother. No one hit him, for which he was grateful, but Rusty had brought Joey with her and handed him to him first thing. He did love this little man.

They must have been having a conversation about him when they left the house because they were still talking about him, he realized, when they showed up at his hotel room. After a few minutes, they brought in food. Mostly Danishes, as well as a couple of gallons of tea. Something that he sorely missed while being here. When they sat down, he held his breath when they all turned to look at him.

"You wouldn't hit a man with a baby, would you?" They just stared at him, and when he held Joey up in front of his face, he asked them if they were in a dangerous mood.

Chapter 2

Caitlynn wasn't really disappointed that Barron's family was around. She liked them, but they were just too pushy for her tastes. She thought, too, that they took advantage of Barron a great deal too. Mostly, it was the women, who she thought could use some lessons in manners but she never said anything to anyone because she wasn't part of the family as yet. Even when she did become a bride of Barron's, she wasn't planning on hanging out with any of them. She was sure that her love for him would hold him back from seeing them so often, too. Christ, they were all grown-ups. It's about time that they left the fucking nests, right?

She had hoped that once Barron had made it to the city to see all the things that he missed living on the mountain that he'd want to move in with her. But he was steadfast in living in the hotel that he'd been in to the point that it irritating her a great deal. Caitlynn supposed that once they fell in love with one another, she'd have a tighter hold over him, but for now, she would go with the flow.

"What do you think of the mountain, Caitlynn? I mean, living there." She most assuredly didn't care for their constant questions about her likes and dislikes. Especially she didn't care for, not hate, but didn't care for Jamie. She asked the other woman what she meant. "You know that someone, one of the Cross men, has to live on the mountain forever in order for them to keep it, correct? It's doubtful to me that any of them would give up living there, but I was curious about your opinion about living there in such a rustic setting."

"It's a nice place to hang out, I suppose. There are plenty of places to go shopping. I do love a good shopping area. I bet it's beautiful this time of year. And what with Thanksgiving coming up next week, you guys probably have a lot of plans made. I'm not used to large crowds of people, so I'm thinking that we'll perhaps skip it this year and be just the two of us, Barron and I, in my apartment. It was just myself and my dad for a long time, then he passed away." Jamie told her that wasn't what she'd asked her. "I'm sorry. I guess I didn't understand. Are you asking me if I would live there all the time? Not if I can help it, no. I don't know that Barron and I have gotten that far in our relationship to make that kind of decision together. It would depend a great deal, I guess, on how often I needed to go back to the city for my business or not. And that wouldn't be for just a day. I'd have to be there for months at a time. I'm sure that none of you have spent a winter here. I hear that it's dangerous. It gets so cold."

"No, none of us women have spent a winter here, but there are furnaces in each of the houses. Also, wood burning stoves in the event the power goes out." Jamie laughed a little. "I do wonder at times what I'll do with myself in the winter months. But I'm not terribly worried. So long as I'm warm and have Mark with me, I think I'll be just fine."

"Do you depend on a man to keep you warm? I don't mean with body heat or anything, but chopping wood and such? I mean, up until this fall, didn't they all work outside the home?" She said that they were all federal agents for the park at one time. "I think I might have known that. Are you trying to pick a fight with me, Jamie?"

"No. Why would you think that? I'm just trying to get to know you, that's all." It was Amelia who asked her why she thought that, too. "I would have thought that you'd had a few questions for us as well. I mean, I had plenty when I found Mark."

"If you're going to be a part of this family, it would be nice to know a bit more about you. I mean, your likes and dislikes. In the event that we go into town, at home, I mean, we'd like to have you enjoy it as well." She flat out told them that she didn't think she and Barron would be spending much time on the mountain; thus, she'd not be spending all that much time with all of them. "Why not? I mean, it's his home? Did he tell you that he didn't want to live there anymore?"

"No. I mean, not in so many words. But he did say that he'd like to have what a big city offered him at times." Amelia told her what else he'd said about his heart belonging to the mountain. "Did he tell you that we'd talked about that? Is that why you know what he said? You shouldn't be listening at key holes, Amelia. It's considered very rude. But in answer to your question about living there. I have a large business to run, and I can't do it online like the rest of you do, if you work at all. I have to be there when a new company comes up for sale so that I can run the numbers and get an answer back to them right away."

"And you don't think that you can do that from the mountain?" She wished that Barron would return. He'd gone out to get them all some food and drinks and left her here. Of course, he had invited her to go along, and she had declined. Now, she wished that she'd gone as well. "Well? Can't you?"

"I don't know that I'd want to do that. I don't want to live on the mountain all the time. To me, it's not so much rustic as it is dirty, and there are a lot of bugs and snakes. I don't mean to say that I have never seen anything like that, but you have to admit that there is a lot of dirt around."

"It's a mountain, not an apartment complex." That statement made her temper flare, but she held onto it. What were they driving at here? She finally, when she was sure that she could talk to them without grating her teeth, asked why they were so concerned as to where she and Barron lived. "He's a part of the family. You too, *if* you're his mate."

"Are you thinking that I'm not?" No one answered her. "Or is it that you're hoping that I'm not. I have news for you guys. I'm not going anywhere. I love the city life. The cabs to get around when I don't want to drive. The grocery stores that aren't fifty miles away. I like having a thermostat that I can turn up or down when I want more heat or cooling. I don't want to have to hunt for my food or dig it up out of the ground to have a nice meal. And if you ask him, I'm betting that Barron will say the same thing. I've been showing him the things that he's missing, and we both have been enjoying ourselves a great deal. We've had dinner every night at a new restaurant. And we could go on having a different cuisine for the next six months if we wanted. And I want to make it clear, it's what *we* want. So, if you have something to say to me or complain about, stop beating around the bush and say it. But know this, Barron is mine, and I don't intend to share him once he puts a ring on my finger."

"Excuse me." She turned to find Barron behind her with his arms loaded with bags. She could smell the Chinese food and nearly told him that she didn't care for it. But, before she could, he spoke to her, his teeth clinched tightly. "I got you a pizza to have as your own meal. I also got some beers to go with dinner. My brothers…my family is coming here too. They're bringing food, too."

He never said a word about what he'd obviously over heard. As the women all grabbed one of the many bags he had on him, they didn't either. Joey was handed off to Barron, and he took him to the other room to change his diaper. There wasn't enough money in the world for her to have done that for anyone's child, not even if he was her nephew or cousin—especially not a child of her own. As they began letting their husbands/mates, whatever they called them, in with more food, she had to go to the kitchen to get a glass of wine. Her temper was out of control by the way they were acting, as if not a single thing had happened while Barron was gone. Well, she'd show them. Even if she had to eat—her body shivered at the thought— an egg roll or something equally nasty to prove to them that she could be a part of the family if she wanted to be. Not that it was going to matter in the long run. They, she and Barron, would live in a big city, and that would be the end of that discussion.

Throughout dinner, no one mentioned the conversation they'd been having. Nothing about her telling them that Barron wasn't going to be going back to the mountain for a long stay. Nor about anything else.

They were laughing and having a good time, leaving her to her own devices as she dug into her pizza. Then she remembered her vow to fit in. They'd made her feel inadequate so far, and she hated that feeling. She turned to the makeshift table to find Barron holding the damned baby again.

"Barron, honey, would you mind letting me have a bit of your egg roll? I want to try some Chinese, too." He told her that they were all gone. But there was some fried rice left. "I'll have some of that. Can you bring it to me?"

"I'll have Mark do it. I'm feeding Joey." She was about as pissed off as she'd been in a while. When Mark handed her a plate full, overmounted amount of fried rice, she wanted to smack him upside the head with it. Instead, she thanked him and put it by her pizza. She picked up the fork that she'd been eating her pizza with and tried to figure out how not to spill it all over her. Rice was tricky like that. "You might like using a spoon better. You can get more rice on it than a fork. I just noticed something. Are you actually eating your pizza with a knife and a fork?"

Caitlynn looked at her pizza and then back at Barron. "How else am I supposed to eat pizza? With my hands? No way. That will be so messy, and the sauce would be under my nails until I can get back into the manicurist until next week. How do you eat it?"

It was Mark that showed her. He just picked up a slice of pizza, folded it in half long ways, and then bit into it. The sauce got all over his chin and face, but he grinned at her while chewing it. Christ, they were pigs. When some of the sauce dripped off his chin and onto her arm, she nearly screamed. But he lifted her arm up and licked the sauce clean. It was all she could do not to puke. As it was, she ran to the bathroom, dry heaving all the way there.

She sat on the floor and laid her head against the wall. Not only had she emptied her belly from her dinner, but she had dry-heaved so much that she knew that she was going to be sore in the morning. When someone knocked on the door, she was happy that Barron had come to see if she was all right. It would have been better had he done it sooner, but disappointment ran through her entire body when she saw that it was Amelia.

"I'm a witch." She had to ask her to repeat that, thinking that she was admitting to being a bitch. But no, she said witch. "I can take the soreness away if you wish. Even the upset stomach, if you would allow it. Want me to help you out?"

"No, I don't want you to help me out. That savage licked my arm." She felt her belly churn again. "Why would he do that?"

"Having a bit of fun? Families do that, you know. Sure, at your expense, but it was just him having some fun." She said she didn't care for that kind of fun. "Yeah, I think we all got that. You're not very amusing, are you? I mean, I'd like to think that sometime later down the line, you might loosen up the rod out of your ass and enjoy hanging around us, but I just don't see that happening. You're sort of set in your ways."

"I'm not set in my ways, but I act like any other person with any kind of manners. Who goes around licking someone like that?" She told her that he was cleaning the sauce off her arm. "Well, why didn't he lend me a napkin or get me a washcloth? I know a great many people, and they have never once licked my arm."

"I got this, Amelia. Thanks for trying." She smiled at Barron when he appeared in the doorway. After sitting in the little area outside of the bathroom, she told him that she was sorry about being sick. But she'd never been licked before. "Yeah. I got that. It's a shame, really. He was making sure, too, that he didn't burn you with the sauce. That's my brother's way of not just trying to get you to have fun but to make sure you weren't burnt either."

"How does that make a difference?" He didn't answer her but did shrug. "You're not like these people, Barron. I hope you know that. They're savages compared to you and I. They were asking me about living on the mountain with you, but I told them just what I thought about that. You and I are alike in thinking that the mountain isn't for us. It's not a place that I'd want to have a family on, either. And speaking of which, I've just decided that I don't want to have children, either. Just the demands that little one here has on everyone would drive me batty. No. I don't want a child or children ever. Neither place is a good place to raise a child. It's dangerous, and I don't know how we'd have time to raise one. Not unless we have full-time help and plenty of full-time nannies. I also decided that I couldn't change a diaper, no matter what was in it."

"All right. You don't want to have children. It's your body, and I'd never force anything like that on you. I'm glad you told me." She smiled at him, knowing that he understood where she was coming from. He didn't speak for several minutes, and she wondered what he was thinking. He was probably thinking about how sorry he was about his family. Well, he should be. "You're not my mate, Caitlynn."

"I'm sorry, what?" He repeated himself, telling her too that they couldn't have children anyway since she wasn't his mate. "Well, I guess that's a good thing. That'll be good for not making any mistakes that we don't want. That's good, right? But we can still have a good life together, right?"

"I want children. A lot of them. But I can see where you won't want any. However, I'd never force you into anything like that, even if we were mates." She asked him how he'd figured out that they weren't mates. "Lots of clues were there, but I was ignoring them. First of all, I don't love you. I like you…well, I thought I might have liked you, but I'm not sure about that either. You've been nothing but rude to my family since they arrived. And when I walked into your conversation with my sisters, I was not happy with the fact that you *think* that you can make me do anything that I don't want to. I'm a grown man, and I make decisions, especially ones that involve my family on my own. Had you been my mate, you would have fit in with the rest of my family. It seemed to me that you didn't even want to try."

"You mean because I don't like them, that makes it so that we can't spend the rest of our lives together? That's the stupidest thing that I've ever heard. You're letting some old folklore decide for you who to love?" He told her that it wasn't folklore but the fates. "Oh well, pardon me for misspeaking. The fates then. I'm not your mate because of some fates decided that we're not. And you're going to allow that to ruin what we have here."

~*~

He didn't answer her. Didn't tell her that they

didn't have anything together. Barron didn't know what to say to her, even if he wanted to answer her. She was pissed off, and he was getting there as well. Instead of dragging out this conversation anymore, he told her that his family had left, but they'd be back tomorrow to take him home.

"You're not staying." He shook his head. "Just like that, you've decided that since I don't get along with your family, then we're not going to be together anymore. Well, that fucking sucks, don't you think? I had it all planned out that we were going to be a couple. Now you're saying because...why? You have to have a reason for just breaking things off with me. Because they told you to? Is that it? They don't like me, so you're going to break it off because of that?"

"I've said this to you before. I'm a grown man." She nodded, then shook her head, telling him that he was a pussy. "Whatever you think about me isn't anything that you can hurt me with anymore. You're not a nice person, and I should have seen that before now."

"I was a nice person until they came along and started accusing me of not loving you." Barron asked her if she did love him. "Yes. With all my heart."

"Well, I don't love you. And I can't be sorry about that, Caitlynn. You've turned into this different person almost overnight. Possessive and mean. I don't care for this real version of you. As I said, I don't even know if I like you right now or not." He got up and started gathering her things. Amelia told him that all he had to do was call out to her, and she'd take Caitlynn home without harming her. And to his way of thinking, they had all wanted to hurt her.

The trash had been cleaned up by his brothers. Everything, all the mess, had fit into two large trash bags. On their way out, they'd taken it all to the lobby for them to toss it out. Mark and the others had left a large tip for the cleaning crew as there was rice on the floor where Caitlynn had been sitting when she got sick. She came out of the bathroom just as he was putting the chairs back at the little table.

"Can we start today over?" He just stared at her. "We got off on the wrong foot today, thanks mostly to your sisters-in-law. I know you call them your sisters, but you do understand that they're not related to you at all, correct?"

"I know that. But they're my sisters as much as my biological brothers are my family. I don't want to be rude here but I would like for you to head back to your place. Enough has been said between us, and I would very much like it if we didn't say something that we'll regret later." She said she thought they'd already gotten there. "All the more reason for you to head back to your place. I'm not going to tell you that I didn't have fun. I did. But it's over."

"But I don't want it to be over, Barron. I want to spend the rest of my life with you." He simply told her no. Barron couldn't think of a better way to let her know that it was finished between them. "No? Just like that? You're willing to throw all that we had away because I don't get along with your family? That's not fair if you ask me."

"I didn't ask you, and yes, I'm willing to toss it all out because you don't get along with my family. They're all I have now that my grandparents are gone. And I trust them." She asked him why he didn't trust her. "Not when I walk into a conversation that you're having, and you've twisted up my words. I never once said that I wasn't going to live on the mountain. I didn't say that I preferred living in the city over what my home has to offer me. You manipulated me and my words to suit yourself. I have decided, because I'm a grown man, that I don't want to see you again. I want nothing to do with you from here on out."

"All right." She found her purse and her sweater where he'd put it for her. Caitlynn didn't want to put it on. He could see her debating about it on her face. Plus, it was already hot out, but it went with her outfit, so he knew that she'd put it on because of that. She looked at him, thinking. "How did they get here so fast? I mean, it took us three hours on a flight to get here. Your brothers brought food here from that stupid mountain, and it was still hot. How did that happen?"

"We own our own private jet. Two, as a matter of fact." She didn't think that was right, but she didn't have enough information just yet to say much. "Also, they've been here for a few days. They missed me as much as I missed them."

Going to the door, she opened it up and stood there staring at him. "This isn't over, Barron. I'm not going to let you just dump me to the side of the road without a fight. You and I were meant to be together, and that's what I want. I usually get what I want, too."

"You can do whatever it is you want, Caitlynn, but not going to allow you to run me down anymore. You go on home and find someone else to love. My heart isn't opened up for you. Perusing this is a lost cause, and you're not going to win."

She slammed the door when she left. Barron let out a long breath he'd been holding and sat down on the closest thing that he found. It just happened to be the chair. Sitting there, he put his head in his hands and rested them on his knees. Feeling like he'd run several miles up a mountain made him exhausted. Just as he was thinking his day couldn't get any worse, he stood up and turned the locks on the door. He did not want her to come back.

It took him an hour to get himself a shower and cleaned up to get to work. His wallet was under the dresser, where he put it when he went to bed last night. Then, from between his mattresses, he pulled out his laptop and plugged it in. Smiling to himself, he wondered what she would have done had she found his wallet and the computer. Barron started thinking of all the things he'd done since he'd come here to hide things from Caitlynn. His head was smarter than his heart had been, and he was happy for it.

After making sure that his orders were still on their way home, he also got online to order more items for the extra goats and cattle he had coming in. The goats liked to play king of the mountain. He'd built a couple of them for the little ones to play on but noticed that they didn't last all that long. After a few trial and errors on his part, he began ordering them from a kids' toy company that made them better and more sturdy. He ordered a set for Joey, too, so that he could play on the slide and swings when he was older. The big balls for the cattle to toss around had been a huge hit last summer, and he was looking forward to seeing if this group played ball, too.

His cell phone ringing had him smiling. Knowing that Roger was going to be calling him soon, he answered with a laugh. Roger said that something had come up and that he needed to talk to him soon.

"If you can have one of your family members bring you here to talk to me, I think that would be perfect." Amelia showed up in seconds, and he found himself standing in Roger Shippley's personal office. "Christ, you have no idea how happy I am to see you all in one piece. We just got the recording of Caitlynn's call at the restaurant. The one right before the man was shot. You're not going to believe what we found."

"Did you find out who the caller was?" Roger said that there wasn't any man. "I'm sorry. I don't understand. She said that he called her, and even your guys said that they heard him. What's going on, Roger?"

"The call came in, that much we can tell. I've several men looking into it now. But the voice on the other end was a recording. The pauses, when she was supposed to talk, were controlled by her." Barron leaned back on the chair he'd sat in when Roger laid a small box with a button on his desk. "Remember that we took her coat, hat, and her phone? Well, she left the device that she was controlling the incoming call in her pocket. She called here about an hour ago asking if we had her garage door opener. That she thought that it was left in her pocket when things went down. They told her that it was still in evidence until they caught whoever had killed the secret serviceman.

That's murder right now at her doorstep."

"Why? I know that you don't know yet as to why she did that, but why would she fake a call like that? Not to mention, how did she rig up the gun so that it shot him in the head when it did?" Barron asked him if he'd had any of his sisters look into this. "I was hoping you'd ask. I'm not sure how much they want me involved in this. Barron, we think the other voice is hers, too. Some of the wording she uses is the same that she does. And like you, I'd like to know what she had hoped to gain by doing this. Aren't you two already an item?"

"No, not after last night." He explained everything that happened and told his good friend how he'd told her to go home. "I'm wondering now if that was such a smart move. Do you think she'll come after me?"

"I'd go home right now if I were you. You know as well as I do that your home is a fortress. And if you don't want her in, she'd not going to get in. Not to mention your sisters and brothers there to protect you." Roger looked as if he had something more to say, so he told him to spit it out. "According to the records that I've been shown, Caitlynn is dead. When we did a search on her name, birthdate, and social, it came up that she died right around the eighteen hundreds. She and her entire family were killed in a train accident. It wasn't until about fifteen years ago that this Caitlynn came to be around and started working with the social that belonged to the dead Caitlynn. Barron, I'm sort of nervous about what else she's done. If she got by us when we did a search on her, I wonder what else we've missed."

Barron reached out to all of his family. After telling them everything that he'd found out from Roger, he told them about the fight that they'd had in the hotel room. He could see his family now, taking notes and making sure that they had the information to dig deeply into her lives, however many she had. But it was Amelia who was going to get the true story behind it all when she dug into Caitlynn's head. Barron didn't doubt either that it would be very painful for the woman too.

"I'll get back to you about whatever I find. I'm not trying to push this off, but it could be a simple thing like this other person is a long-lost relative. No, that won't work. The social. Christ, I'll get back to you guys."

He talked to Roger some more, showing him the pictures of Caitlynn when she was about eighteen and having nothing more. There were no school records, and nothing was saying that she graduated from school or college. Barron was suddenly more afraid of her than he'd been at the hotel.

Chapter 3

Mark was glad that he'd had their living room enlarged. The reading of the will at his home made it cozy but very open. He didn't know why, but it felt better being read at his homestead, but it just did. It was his family, after all and he didn't want to miss out on a moment to be with them. He missed his grandparents every day and had to stop a couple of times a day from going to find them to tell them something. All of his brothers had said the same thing. They missed them terribly.

All the women were dressed in dresses or skirts. Each of his brothers had worn nice jeans and a good tie. It made him smile that they had all, without encouragement from anyone, decided to look nice for the last thing that they'd do for them.

Christ, he missed them both so much that, at times, he had to find him a quiet corner and sob in. Mark did wonder if it ever got any easier.

"We're going to have to go over your grandfather's will first. As you know, he was killed first, and the way he met his demise will make a huge difference in the way that the insurance pays off." They all nodded and told Mr. Shapley that they understood. "Good. I have to tell you, I never dreamed that when I wrote this up for them all those years ago, I'd be talking to you six grown men so many years later. Especially being that they're both gone at the same time. They were... there are no words that I can say that can convey how much they meant to this old man. They were the best thing that ever happened to this park. Now. Let me begin."

It was just as they had thought it would be. Grandda left all his insurance money to Grannie. But if in the event that she had already passed on, it would go to his grandsons. Mr. Shapley explained that he'd have to come back to that when he was finished with the entirety of the wills.

There were also the treasures that Grandda wanted them to have. A corncob pipe that his father had made for him. A neck tie that he wore to church on Sunday. Other items that would mean something profound to the one that he left it to. When he was at the end of the list, Mr. Shapley picked up a second sheet of paper. He could see that it was hand written and even that the paper was yellowed with age. Putting his hand over his heart, he needed just a moment to think about what this might mean to his family that was left.

"This is a revision that was sent later to me for the great-grandchildren that would come along after he was gone. I do believe that Thad was the one that got him started on it. He wants Mark to make sure that each grandson gets one of the many carving knives that he made. He said that you'd be the one who would figure out when the young man was old enough to receive it. I do believe with all my heart that he never, well, neither of them expected to live for as long as they did. Can you imagine how many changes they've seen in their long lifetime? It boggles the mind."

"I'll take care of that for them. I'll hand them over to my brothers when their children come along that way, they'll be able to teach them, just the way that we were on how to use them." Mr.

Shapley was good with that, and he picked up Grannie's will.

"Your grannie had a bit more than your grandda did. Not just in money, there was a great deal of that, but there were the things that she had before they wed that your grandda made sure were hers to distribute the way she wanted." Mr. Shapley had to excuse himself to blow his nose. The poor man was more emotional than they were. "I'm sorry. Grannie has here that she wanted her stores, I'm to understand that there were several of them were to go to the brides of her boys. Meaning you grandsons. Also, any proceeds that you make in the store that goes to you ladies as well. She told me that every woman needs a bit of pocket money, and she wanted you to spend the money on yourself."

"Oh my, that's very generous of her." The women hugged, talking about how wonderful that was of her to do that. Shapley said that there was a list of the stores. He'd made them copies of the stores, and Mark could see as well as what the yearly income had been over the last few years. There were indeed seven of them, including the big store that everyone had a part in.

"I don't believe at the time of the writing of this will there were any wives to you young men so she said that the women would figure it out when they came. She also said that it would be like she'd just slipped out one day, and they were there. It would be a perfect match for a lady to sell at their stores." Shapley blew his nose again. "Your grandparents? They're the best I've ever worked with."

Mark needed a small break and was glad that their cook had suggested putting out platters of sandwich-making things. There was also a veggie platter that he enjoyed, and he couldn't help but laugh a little at what Caitlynn might have said about digging out the veggies to eat. He'd done that very thing, digging around in the cellar to get some of the carrots that he needed to be reminded of his grannie. He didn't mention it to his brothers, it wasn't the time, but he was going to have to talk to Barron later about what was going to happen with the woman. She was dangerous if she started coming around and making demands.

The half-hour break was just what he needed. It seemed to him that it had been for everyone. His brothers, joking around with each other, seemed to be in a much better mood, and Mr. Shapley didn't seem to be as upset as he'd been when he broke things up for a bit. After they were all seated, he picked up another file.

"All right, everyone. The insurance that your grandfather had when the park opened all those years ago had a rider on it that stated if he was killed on the job, and according to the fine print, it looks like they took precautions about who would be the one that killed him, that if it had been one of the wild animals, his insurance would have doubled. The second rider would have tripled it if he had been killed by a landslide, tree falling, or an accident while the mountain was covered in bad weather." Shapley looked up at them. "Your grandfather added these next parts just after your father was born. You have to remember that back then, the park was brand new and still finding its feet, and they were more than happy to let him and your grannie fix up their wills, just in case. He made a good point that if something like that were to happen, it would no less hurt the young family — a large family left behind. He went on to say that finding the body might well have been difficult or next to impossible in the type of jobs that he held.

However, since he was killed by a visitor, which I must say no one would have thought of but your father — I suppose because he was an insurance agent, that the policy was to have been multiplied five times the amount."

"I'm sorry. Five times? I don't want to sound greedy or anything, but are you sure that's right?" Shapley told them all how he'd gone to the main office to see if they were going to honor that amount. "I'm assuming since you're telling us that they agreed."

"Not only did they agree, young man, but they didn't even ask me what the original amount was. Had they, I'm sure, I'm almost sure that they would have negotiated a different settlement for the six of you." He laughed a little. "Your grandparents were the oldest living park volunteers as well as the ones who had been here the longest. I believe that they were looking at those numbers when they decided to honor their agreement. Also, you might want to know there was no one else who had their insurance policy enhanced like your parents did, so it would be a great amount. They were smart. I will tell you what they did. Even going as far as being killed by the job, which your father was as well, the policy was more than any other payout that I'd come across, too."

"What you've not said to us, and I'm almost afraid to ask, is that our mother did the same thing, didn't she?" He nodded at Barron. "I'm only guessing here, and if you feel the need to correct me, give me a minute or two—the policies were for over a million dollars by themselves. Before anyone started tweaking them. Correct?"

"Yes, you're correct." Shapley laughed, then put his hand over his mouth before speaking again. "Each one of you are named in the policies as getting the same amount. Fifty-million each. Then the policies are ten times when you count your mothers and fathers tweaking." Shapley laughed again, sort of like he was slightly overwhelmed. "It's the largest payout in any policy to date that I've ever had to pay out, as I said. But we haven't even gone over your grandmother's policies yet."

"I think that...why don't we take another breather to think about Grannie's policies." Mark looked around the room and then back at Shapley. "Is it going to be another billion dollars?"

"Yes." Mark stood up, and then he left the room. From the kitchen, he could hear the others talking, and he started to sing. He had a tune in mind, but the words escaped him. So, as he made up words to go with his little ditty, he decided that he would never, for so long as he lived, ever think about money again. He added that to his song, too.

"We have money now. A great deal of it. Not that we didn't before, but now we have too much. I hope no one finds out. Here, Bossy, did you want a bite of ham? I can afford to give it all to you." The cat, his grannie's cat, didn't touch the ham he'd dropped but did look at him oddly. "You wouldn't have that look on your face if you knew what I knew. But then, you might—"

"Mark?" He looked at his brother Ewing, and he knew that he must have looked a fright. "You're scaring the women. Not to mention the rest of us. Please, come and sit down with us—"

"I don't think so. I think I'm going to float right off my rocker and sing a song about it. I bet people will pay me for it, too." He thought about the two billion they were each going to get now and smiled again. "I think later I'm going to go down to the ice cream parlor and have all the ice cream I want. I don't even—Ouch! You slapped me. What was that for?"

"You're off your rocker. Go into the living room and have a seat." He told his brother he wanted a sandwich. "All right. I'll bring it to you. You're scaring your wife."

Mark made his way to his wife. She didn't smack him, as he thought that she would, but she did hold his head to her breast. Now that he was calmer, as calm as he could be, Mark decided that they were going to have to get them a full-time attorney to make sure that they were all right with their taxes when the time came around. He was glad when everyone decided to stay for dinner. He didn't know if celebrating was going to happen, Mark thought they were all in shell shock, but they would have fun.

~*~

Willow watched the two men who were setting bear traps from her high position in the tree. As soon as they were out of sight, she'd climb down and snap the traps so they'd not work. She'd been doing this for the last four years, and it was getting harder and harder to find them unless she, like today, was able to see them doing it. It wasn't just illegal but it was dangerous too.

Just as she was climbing down the tree

she'd been in for the last hour, she saw the big bear coming up the mountain. She could tell that he was a shifter. There were a great many of them around the mountains it seemed. Just her luck, the big lummox was going to get his foot taken off because his timing sucked. She watched as closely as she could until she had no choice but to speak to the shifter.

"Don't move." When he stopped, she smiled. It would have been a beautiful picture had she had a camera the way he was poised there with his one paw up and his other just a scant inch from the rusty bear trap in front of him. *"Since I can tell you're a shifter, I want you to back up — without lowering your paw about a foot. Can you do that?"*

"I can wiggle back, I think, but I'm fearful of dropping my hand. It seemed important to you that I didn't move my hand." She told him not to move. She was coming to save him. *"I'm not sure what you're saving me from, but you have no idea how much I appreciate this. I've had a really shitty couple of weeks. Some good to it, but for the most part it's — "*

"Do you babble all the time like this? If so, someone should have pointed out to you that it's fucking annoying when shit is about to hit the fan." He didn't

speak again. When she was standing in front of him, he looked at her face. *"That is the best costume I've ever seen anyone wearing. It looks authentic."*

She had to think about what she was wearing but looked down at herself. She had on knee-high moccasins that were lined with wool. A long shirt, like the moccasins made by the skin of a buffalo. Her coat, almost too heavy for the nice weather that they were having, was made of bear skin and fit her a bit too large. She had done that so that she could wear it for a couple more winters before having to find herself another fallen bear. The tribe that she lived with was under the assumption that no animal was left to rot if there were parts. This time, the skin could be used for their well-being.

"It is. I live with a couple of the tribes here in the mountains. They've taught me how to survive in this hard life we have here." She told him not to move while she walked away to find something to snap the trap. When she came back, she had a large log in her hand and looked at the bear. "All right. I wasn't going to tell you until I did it, but you're too close. There is a bear trap about half an inch from your right paw. Or hand, whatever you call it. I'm going to spring it, but it's going to pop up off the ground a little. Not to harm you unless it bloodies your mouth, but it won't snap on you. Just stand still."

"*Count.*" She asked him what he said. "*Could you count to three or something? You know, just to give me a heads up?*"

She simply slammed the log into the trap. It did pop up and hit him on the bottom of his mouth, and it hurt, but if he'd put his paw down, he would have lost it. The thing is meant to take off the paw to capture the animal.

"*You didn't count.*" She told him he was surprised, which was better. "*I suppose. I'm going to shift. Can you turn your back or something? I have clothing, but I need to stop my mouth from bleeding.*"

"Do whatever you need to do. I have to follow the two men that are setting these suckers. This is the fifth one that I've snapped this week following them." She started away and wasn't surprised when the big bear ran up beside her. "I thought you were going to go nurse your mouth."

"*I want to keep you safe. You saved my life, and I need to keep you out of harms –* "

"At what part in my saving your life did it look like I couldn't take care of myself? I mean, really? I was all right just letting you snap your foot off and walking away, but I thought you'd put up a big ruckus and draw the men back here. You're big enough to cover a large area if they wanted you for a rug." She stopped at the top of the hill and laid on her belly. He did the same, scooting himself up so that he could see into the valley like she was. "Is there anything that I can do to get you to go away?"

"Nope." He looked over the hillside, and she was surprised at how many people were there. *"How long have they been down there? It looks like it's been a while."*

"Two weeks, the best I can figure." Her whispered answer had him looking around to see if anyone was close to them. "If you look up there in the mountain about two hundred yards from the campfire, you can see that they got a bear before I found them. I've already figured out how to get the cubs to the forest rangers so they'd not die, too. I know that it's against the laws of nature to do that, but there are a lot of them left behind thanks to these people, and I love the bears most of all. No one will know that I did it. Understand?"

"Yes, I won't say anything." He watched the

men, pissed off that they had their families there with them doing such a dangerous thing. *"You said you have been tracking them for four years. Do they come back yearly, or is it a different group each time. That would help when I let the rangers know."* She was using a pair of binoculars. *"Tell me what you're seeing, please?"*

"There are fifteen men with rifles. Ten of the men are barely out of high school. I don't know why, but I have a feeling this is one of those becoming a man kind of bullshit. The Cherokees know that they're here, but so long as they don't murder for fun, they pretty much leave them alone. However, when they found out they were using bear traps, they've been sending out men to help me find them. It's my thing, you see." She moved the glasses from the group at the bottom. "If you shift now, I won't look at you. I have no desire to see any more naked men than I have already."

Willow felt the air tighten around her, taking her breath away. When the man reached for her glasses, she pointed up the hill about halfway up. She knew when he saw the tribe.

"They won't kill them. Unless they fire on them first. Which I think is going to happen regardless. The tribe will tie them up, put out their fires, and destroy their camp gear. The bear will be dragged away so that other animals can have a meal from the carcass. Usually, they'd take the meat and smoke it, but they don't trust what the white men have done to it." There was a single rifle go off, and it didn't look to her like anyone was fatally hurt. "They'll notify the rangers by the way of cell phone and let them know where they are. Usually, they let them sit for a few hours just to teach them a lesson."

"Do you know what will happen to the kids?" She said that she'd not given it any thought before. "I don't know that I would have either, now that I think about it."

When he handed her back the binoculars, she thanked him. Then she noticed that he was dressed. Thanking him for coming with her, she told him that she was headed back to the tribe. He didn't move when she did.

"My name is Barron Cross. My family has lived on this mountain for generations. Have you heard of us?" She told him that all the tribes up in the deep mountains knew who Alford and Minnie Cross were. "My grandparents. Did you hear that they died recently?"

"Yes. The tribes here paid tribute to them for ten days and ten nights when they heard. There are markers, if you know what to look for all through the park about them. If I see you again, and one is near, I'll show it to you. They were good people, your grandparents, and saved a great many Indians when they came to them for help. Your grandda, he was kind to everyone, and when he found things, artifacts that he would find while out, he would ask the chief if he could let the white man see them." He asked her if she was a white woman. "I am. They raised me when they found me wandering the park. I was seven then. I've been living and being with them for the last eighteen years or so."

When she pulled her balaclava off her head, her dark red hair flew all over the place in the slight breeze coming from the gully that the people were in. He stared at her face. She knew what he could see. Dark freckles that bloomed when she was out of doors for more than a few minutes, as well as her clear blue eyes. They were as crystal clear blue as the sky was when the sun shined over it, as she'd been told by Chief Roanhorse, her adopted father.

He stood up when she did, as she turned away, thinking that she'd had enough of him for one day, he asked her if she'd come and meet his family. Have dinner with them. Then he smiled.

"I'd very much like it if you were to tell them what you told me about your tribe and my grandparents. They would enjoy that as much as I have. Please." She looked at the way that her home was. It wasn't anything more than a hole in the mountain while she was out. Tomorrow, she would return to the tribes that she lived with. Finally, Willow told him that she'd be honored so long as she was able to leave when she needed to. She and the Cherokee were very close. "That'll be great. All right. Thank you."

As they started down the mountain again, she asked if they needed any honey. She'd been out checking on her trees and had gotten more than she could handle. Handing him one of the gallons of the pure gold stuff, she took the other. Her tribe had more than they could use right now, too.

~*~

Barron was beyond happy. He almost didn't want to shift to talk to her because he didn't want to be disappointed when he was naked again. But not only was he fully clothed lying beside her, but he also had on a winter coat and heavy boots. He nearly did a dance. He'd been so happy.

He supposed that he should have told her what she was to him. However, he was a little nervous. First of all, she had a blade on her hip that was as large as his head. There were other weapons around her, too, that he knew that she could use on him at a moment's notice. But as they walked toward his home, Mark's home, all he could think about was that he'd found his mate, and she was nothing like the other woman. Glancing at her, he realized that he knew absolutely nothing about her. He asked her what her name was.

"Willow. I don't remember my last name. I didn't even remember my first name, but my biological father called me Willow all the time. When we arrived here on a family vacation, it was...complicated. My father had joined a cult. One that he had us following all across the United States when my family and I were little. I was seven at the time." He asked her if she would wait and tell his family her story. "Do you really think that they'll care? I mean, I don't anymore. I got free of them, and that's a good thing."

"I'm sure that they'll be happy to hear the story about how you'd come to be living with a tribe. I'm assuming by the way you talk that they abandoned you. We have that happen a bit more than I'm comfortable with by living here. At one time, I was a park ranger, along with the rest of my family." She said she knew a great deal about his family. "I would imagine that you did if you knew about my grandparents. I have to tell you something before we go in and meet my family. You know that there are six of us, correct?"

"Yes. The oldest is the bear king. What else?" He in stops and starts told her about Caitlynn. Also, that she would more than likely be making trouble for him and his family. And now her. "Why me? I've—" She cocked her head at him. "You're saying that you're my mate, aren't you?"

"I belong to you, yes. You're my true mate." She continued walking, and he didn't say much but stayed at pace with her. "Are you upset?"

"No. Flabbergasted but no, not upset. I believe in the fates and their way of working things out as much as you do. But I am still a little scared, too." She stopped, and he did, too. Turning to look at him, she studied his face like she was looking for flaws. "I can take care of myself. I'm a warrior as much as the men in my tribe. I have been adopted by the chief when he found me injured and dying one day. I think that I'd been in the forest for about a week by then. After nursing me back to health, he claimed me as his child."

"I'm sure that there is a reason that you're telling me this, but I can't think of a reason why it should matter. I'm not being a dick here, but I don't know the ways of the Indians that live here in the mountains. I know there are several tribes, but nothing more than that." She nodded, then continued to walk at a pace that had him lengthening his stride to keep up with her. "Are you upset about this?"

"No. Why would I be?" He said that he didn't know, but she did seem to be. "I'm speaking to my father. He would like to meet you. He's going to be at your brother's home before we will be. I don't know what he's going to ask of you. Tradition is huge with him. You will need to show that you can provide for me. Not just in monetary ways but just to keep me safe. Why? I have no idea. I've been taking care of myself for decades. But it's his tradition and he'll expect something from you to claim your life to mine." She looked at him. "Showing him your bear will be enough. But you'll be bigger, stronger, too, if we were to claim one another. Would you do that? Before we meet him?"

"Anything. You tell me what you need for me to do to claim you." Her face heated up, and he laughed. "We have to have sex? I'm more than willing to make love to you whenever you say that word."

"Just a kiss will do for now." He pulled her to his body and let her decide how close she wanted to be to him. As he lowered his mouth to hers, she let out a soft breath, just enough for him to taste her. Claiming her mouth, it was so much more than he could ever have hoped for and then some. Barron had a mate, and he couldn't have been more in love with her than he'd been in love with anyone else.

Chapter 4

Caitlynn tossed the book she'd been reading across the room. It was drivel, and she wasn't any closer to figuring out why she wasn't his mate than she'd been before. In her lifetime, she'd been several fiancées to her fiancés, and not once had any one of them meant a thing to do with her loving them until the next big prize came alone. She wanted to be his mate in the worst sort of way. He was handsome, friendly, and, most importantly, he was rich. It hadn't taken her as long as she thought it should have to figure that part out as it did to read one of the several hundred books that were out there on shifters. It seemed to her that she should have been setting her sights on shifter men rather than plain old men. Shifters seemed to know how to collect money and to keep it, just for little old her. She laughed as she thought of how sincere Barron was — his name even sounded rich when he'd had to break it off with her.

The books would go from saying that there wasn't any such thing as shifters to having about every other man or woman being one. They were just that good at keeping their shape-shifting a secret. Christ, the only real information that she could find was by reading those ridiculous smut books. Even those only talked about sex and how wonderful it was when they came together. She also found out, through reading up on getting with child by one was that ovulation wasn't two weeks like Barron had told her but only a few hours once a month. That pissed her off more than anything.

Her phone was ringing, and she decided to ignore it for now. The business was doing well, even without the expansion she was hoping to get, so she had very little to do with it. In fact, as bored as she was with the company, she'd gone ahead and did what she should have done years ago. Putting it on the market to get rid of it was the best decision she'd ever made. There were other fish to fry, as her father used to say.

He'd nearly bankrupted them when he'd been in charge. Dad had wanted to branch out, of course, but he wanted to take on more smaller companies, up-and-coming ones that he thought would be a good investment to their company. After he told her this, she decided that he was much too easy with the company and declared him incompetent to run the place. A few weeks later, she won the case through the board of directors, and he died of a massive heart attack. Then, her mother, who was about as useless as any woman could be, joined him in death by taking her own life. Good riddance to the both of them, she had thought then and now.

Her secretary knocked once and said that there were several messages for her from the service. Asking her if anything was important enough that she had to stop what she was doing, she told her that it wasn't her job to judge on that sort of thing people wanted her for. Handing her the missed call papers, she left the room without another word. Caitlynn wanted to fire her, but she did a good job in keeping her abreast of things and didn't want to have to hire someone else this late in the game. She started sorting through the messages.

Two were from her banker, telling her that they had a buyer for the business, and that made her smile. The next three were from her butler telling her that there were several messages from someone wanting to put an offer on the business. He then asked if they'd all be out of a job.

"You might well be if you ask shit like that." After calling her banker to find out what sort of offers they were getting, he, of course, started telling her that since he'd left the second message, his phone hadn't stopped ringing.

"I wish you would have told me that I was going to be getting calls like this, Ms. Royce. I would have had the phone calls transferred to your system instead of taking up my time answering questions that I know nothing about." She asked him what the offers were. "All of them are less than what you're asking with the exception of one. What do you know of someone known as David Gibb? He's willing to pay the full asking price if he could have the buildings as well as keep all the employees that are there now. He also wants to close within the next three weeks."

"Did he say what the rush was?" He told her

when she asked. "So he doesn't want me fucking with the employees before he takes over. Not very trusting of him if you ask me."

"That isn't the wording that he used, no, but I guess it boils down to that. What do you want me to tell him? He's been calling here for the last few hours on the dot to see if you're willing to meet him to get the paperwork signed over to him as soon as the day's end." She looked at her calendar and then called in her secretary to see when her next free time was. After being told that she had nothing on her calendar for the next three days, she told her banker that. "Today, then?"

"Why not? I don't want this drawn out any longer than he does. I want money not some excuse for him telling me that he doesn't have the money right now. It's pay up, or I move on to the next person." He reminded her that there wasn't a next person who was willing to pay what she wanted. "I know that, dumbass. I want you to tell him that I have several offers on the table. I want him to squirm a little."

He said he'd call her back and decided to look up this David Gibb person. All she could find out about him was that his wife of thirty-one years had died recently and that he'd been staying with friends. It never mentioned who his friends were, but she had noticed that his house, like a lot of houses on the market in DC, was somewhat of a mansion with an indoor swimming pool and bar all in one. She thought that it must be some house if he was asking eleven million for the place. There were no records that she could look up on him or his wife. The friends part didn't bother her. She wouldn't have mentioned it either if she'd been hiding out from someone. The press.

Glancing through the phone messages that she'd gotten, three of them were from newspapers around the state wanting to talk to her. Whatever. She didn't have anything to say to them that she'd not already said when she put the business on the market. Cailynn had decided too to get rid of the house that she'd been living in since she was a child. It was time to start fresh, she thought. And to do that, she needed to get Barron off his ass and ask her to marry him. She wanted to live in the style that he could give to her. She didn't want to work at all for the rest of her life. The buzz of the phone startled her, and she was told by whatever her secretary's name was that it was her banker.

"He said that he could meet you at this bank in twenty minutes. Also, he is bringing his attorney with him." She asked him if she should bring one with her. "How well do you know that law pertaining to selling a company?"

"I don't know anything about it. So I'm asking if I should bring one, not how much I know." He told her that she might well have one there in the event she had a few legal questions, but other than that, he could help with some answers. "I'm selling. How hard can that be? All right. I'm going to depend on you so that I don't get fucked over. I'll be leaving the office now."

Before leaving, however, she called the realtor about her home. The staff was going to show her around since she had already made arrangements that she could do it all today and then called her butler, whatever his name was, to tell him that she was selling the house as well. All he said to her was very good, ma'am, and then he asked if there was anything else. She wanted him to ask if they were going to be out of a job, but he didn't. So she didn't say anything. Maybe this guy, this Gibb person, needed a home too. She was going to mention that as well. The realtor was going to call her as soon as she had a price worked out, and Cailynn was thrilled more than she had been when she realized that Barron had a great deal of money. While she wasn't going to live in that godforsaken mountain range, they should be looking for a home together. Something that she picked out. He had the taste of a barbarian because of where he lived now, and he wasn't even going to be able to pick out the lamps in their own home. There is no telling what he'd want. Antler lamps or something. Not that some people liked them, she supposed. But she didn't want so much as a bug in their home, stuffed or not.

She arrived at the bank a few minutes later than she had planned on. The woman who was going to sell her home said that she'd be out there today to have a look around and had about a million questions about the furniture and curtains and if they were a part of the house.

"Yes, of course. Everything goes but the desk in my dad's office. That will come with me." She knew that it had treasures inside of it but hadn't figured out how to get it open yet, so she thought that she could at least look to see what sort of shit he'd left in it. It wasn't a deal breaker, so she asked for a price with and without the oversized desk. Then she hung up on her, telling her that she was headed to a meeting.

The banker had led her to a large conference room. Mr. Gibb, David he asked her to call him. He had his attorney with him, and she wished as soon as she saw him that she'd had one, too. The table was lopsided looking, with just her on one side and the two men on the other. She kept staring at the attorney like she thought that she had used him before.

"Do I know you? I mean, have we done business together?" The attorney said that he didn't know her at all, and no, they'd not done any sort of business together. "You look like someone that I should know. Whatever. Oh, I just put my house on the market, too, if you're interested. I want myself and my fiancé to start fresh and I think that living in the house that I own now will put a damper on things. So, if you're in the market for a five-bedroom home, my realtor is there now, figuring out how much it's worth. I can't imagine that it will be too much. It's as old as the hills my boyfriend used to live on."

"Your fiancé used to live on the mountains,

you say? That's so odd because that's where I live, too." She said that they had to stay there in order to keep the park from taking the land back. "I remember that rule. Don't you, Roger? It's called the grandfather law from some years—"

"I don't want to be rude or anything, but I'm here to talk business. You said that you were willing to pay what I'm asking for the building with a few stipulations. I'm fine with whatever you wish. I just want to get out from under it and be a wife of leisure. He's very wealthy." Roger, the attorney, handed her a sheath of papers. After looking it over quickly, she was satisfied, too, that it had a check pinned to the front of it for the entire asking price. She looked at her banker. "Did you read this over?"

She had to ask him twice so that he'd answer her. Finally, when he did, he actually laughed, telling her that there were few attorneys that he would trust as much as this man. Caitlynn didn't know what the hell he was talking about but was so happy that the check was right there. All those zeroes made her kind of giddy.

Signing where the little pink and blue tabs were, she waved the banker off when he started to explain to her what she was signing. The check, she knew, was causing her to be hasty, but that was all right, too. She was going to put this money away, and in the event that Barron left her for some reason, she could have some fallback money of her own.

Just as they were finishing up with the signatures that were needed, the realtor called. Nearly not answering it, just to bask in the check for a bit longer, she did. No one moved when she told them who it was, and she stepped into the hall to listen to what she had to say.

"It needs a great deal of work. Were you aware of that?" She told her that was the very reason she was selling it. "I thought as much. If you wait and have the kitchen redone, as well as a roof replacement, you could get a considerable amount of money for the house and contents. The leaving of the desk doesn't add or take away much in the value of the home. In fact, since it's going to be difficult to move whoever takes it, I'm sure that you'll have to lessen your price by several thousand dollars so someone can have it removed. It must weigh about several thousand pounds, being as it is in four pieces that would have to be taken apart to get out—"

"How much is it worth? I might just be able to sell it right now, too." She told her. It was much more than she thought that she'd get for the old place, but she was happy that it wasn't less. "All right. Good then. Are you going to be in your office for a bit more? I don't want to have to wait until tomorrow to get a fat paycheck and maybe him changing his mind. All right?"

"Yes, of course. I'll be here until I hear from you. It's only one now, so I can start on the paperwork while I'm waiting." She told her that was an excellent idea. "All right. I'll call you soon."

Taking a deep breath, she walked into the office. The men were talking, probably about their latest woman escapades, and she ignored it for having a seat. After telling the Gibb person how much the price was, he sat there for several seconds to what she thought was in thought. Christ, this was so easy. She might well go to Barron her luck was so good right now. He might be missing her about now.

"I'll take the house, but I'm not willing to pay that much. From what I've heard, the place needs not just a new roof, but the kitchen dates back to the fifties. It will be difficult to have anyone fix a meal for myself if they had to use it. There are carpets throughout the house that are nearly as old as it is. The walls will need to be stripped down and redone. That's going to cost a fortune to have fixed up even before I move into it." She asked him what he was willing to pay. Caitlynn nearly fell off her chair when he said that exact amount that she'd been wanting to get, knowing that it was a fixer-upper. "If you're in agreement with that, I'll sign the paperwork now to get you paid."

"Deal." She couldn't control her laughter. The man was a fool if he thought that he'd gotten a good deal on the house. It was a great deal less than the realtor had mentioned. She'd wanted to sell it for four hundred thousand. The price that she wanted was fifty-five grand. Since that was what she wanted, Caitlynn decided that she'd just cut her losses and sell it. She'd made a killing off the business, too.

After a certified check was given to her. She looked at the amount of money that she had in her possession and laughed. Mr. Gibb, or whatever his name was, asked if he could take possession now as she was leaving the furniture behind. As she didn't want anything from the house, including her clothing, she told him it was his as of the moment that he'd handed over the check. She did have to sign another sheath of papers saying he was buying it as is, but she didn't care for the loss of a few things when she knew that with all her money, she could buy whatever she wanted from now on.

After the attorney for Gibb left, the banker, she figured that she should learn his name. Mr. David Rugby helped her get her paperwork in order so that she'd have the lesser amount in the bank now. He told her that he wasn't the normal banker of this place but was helping out a friend when this came about.

Like she cared. She asked him if the money was good, and not only did he say it was, but he also told her that she'd have to let the bank know thirty days in advance if she was going to put the larger check in her account. Their insurance only covered two hundred-fifty thousand in any single person's account.

"Yeah, whatever. I'm going to have me a nice dinner, then go and talk to Barron. He'll be so happy that I'm doing this for us. I doubt very much

he'll care where we live so long as we're together."
He told her that he'd read in the paper about Barron
Cross lately, but he couldn't remember what it
was about. "It's more than likely the engagement
announcement that I wrote up. He and I are going
to be so happy together."

Caitlynn was so excited she nearly forgot that
she'd come to the bank in a limo. There were going
to be more rides like this one, she told herself. She
was never going to have to drive anywhere again.
Just as she was getting into the limo, she realized
that it didn't belong to her anymore and asked
the driver to take her home. Surely Gibb wouldn't
begrudge her getting some clothing until she got
her some new things.

~*~

Willow laughed every time she thought of the
stupid woman. The man Gibb was at the bank
representing the banker would have been running
windows for the time being while he paid bills and
cashed checks. The president and vice president
had been the buyers for them. She and Barron and
the attorney for them just for fun. She had to laugh
every time she thought of Caitlynn asking the
president of the free world if she knew him. What

a dumb crack.

Just as they had thought Caitlynn would do, she didn't read any of the paperwork but signed at the tabs where told. Then when she decided to sell the house and contents without reading that contract, Mark made a few calls on their behalf to have the locks changed on the house and the windows reinforced so she couldn't break them. Amelia had, with her magic, made it so that instead of breaking, it would call the police to let them know that the house was trying to be broken into. She'd be arrested on the spot if she did that.

Being at the homestead was like being with the tribe. The house, of course, was different and not a lean-to. She and the chief had a nice teepee that they shared, large enough for the two of them to have as much room as they needed. Since it had been snowing a little today, she knew that Father would be keeping the leather walls so warm that snow wouldn't dare drop on it for knowing that it wasn't long for the world. It made her smile every time she thought about her father when she'd told him that she was mated to one of the Cross bears.

He had arrived just after she and Barron had to Mark's home. If he was surprised to see the eight great ponies that Father had brought along with several blankets and foodstuffs, Barron nor anyone in his family said a word. Mark, like the rest of his brothers, was born to the mountains and would know, even if it was just a little bit of the ways of the tribes. The bears, the Cross bears, had been here longer than most. The tribes, this one, her tribe, in particular, had been here a great deal longer than they had. Even longer than their grandparents.

They were laughing at the stupidity of the woman named Cait Lynn—how her father pronounced it. After getting things settled about the house and business, the two of them, her and Barron, decided it might be a good thing if they were to go to the offices of the businesses they'd purchased in the morning. It was then that her father stood.

"I will honor you much as I would have if Willow were a child of my body. You are aware that she is not of my blood but closer to me than even my sons before they were killed." Everyone told him that they were sorry. Willow introduced her father to the men and women in the room. When she came to Mark, she told him that he was the king of all bears and that his brothers were just as honorable as he was. "I have found that out myself. These are good men, the six of them. And when your grandparents passed, it was as if a great wall had come tumbling down on my heart and soul. I was so aggrieved by their passing. The forest itself had mourned that day and daily since their loss was so great, too."

"Thank you, sir. You've no idea how good that makes me feel. The bears had come to us that night. All of them, shifter and bear alike, came to pay homage too. That meant a great deal to all of us, but this, you honoring me with your presence and telling me that you hurt when they passed, means a great deal to me and my family as well." Mark was asked to get down on his knees with the rest of his brothers and their wives, with the exception of her and Barron. "You've no need to give us anything, sir. We're—"

Willow kicked him in the foot and told him to hush. After a short burst of laughter, he did just that. Once her father started talking again, he told them of the temperament of his only child. That wasn't as funny to her as it was for the rest of them but they did pay attention.

"I give to you and your family eight ponies. It is for the seven years that my daughter suffered at the hands of her biological parents. They were beyond cruel to one so young, and we have, our tribe, have taken her into our hearts and have never once regretted a moment of it. Now that she's met her mate in a Cross, everything that I had a dream about has come true. She will, along with Barron Cross, be the best for this mountain." Father laughed a little. "Barron might regret her temperament once in a while, but she does have a good heart."

No one said anything, but they did laugh. They were told to bow their heads as he was going to give them their gift.

"I give to you the tribes that have been in these mountains since they were discovered as a good source of food and water for us. There are nearly seven thousand strong people, and I am the chief of all of them. The park leaves us alone for the most part, and we have become stronger for it." Mark looked up but lowered his head again. "You might well have guessed that I'm much older than I appear. Much like your witch here, I have been around these mountains for longer than man came over on the ships to claim the land that was not theirs to claim. I pass this magic on to you. You do have immortality already, but my magic will keep you all around for longer than these mountains have been here. You will see things that no other man will foresee. You will be, from now on, alive at any cost."

It was Barron who asked how that was different than the immortality they had now. Willow smiled and said that they couldn't be killed, not even by removing their heads. Nothing would poison them, such as iron or silver. They were what shifters called true immortals and would be in these mountains so long as they took care of the earth and all its creatures.

"You'll be able to speak to all the animals that live here too. Not just shifters but all forms of animals and creatures." Mark thanked her for clearing it up. "Barron can already speak to the earth. He has been able to since his birth. Not that I think he is aware of it, but he will be a better caretaker for the world because of it. You all will be able to do the same. And use it for the betterment of the world around us."

"I don't mean to be stupid, but once they're

given this magic, what will happen to Willow and me? I mean, you've singled us out for a reason, I'm guessing." Father laughed and told him that he had the gifts of the earth the moment that he kissed his daughter. "Oh. Usually, a person receiving magic like that gets knocked on their ass. Why didn't I feel it? Or is there more to it than that?"

"There is no reason for you to suffer needlessly. You have accepted Willow into your heart, and that is as good as it gets." Her father looked toward the door to the front of the house. "The person Caitlynn will arrive here in the next few days. You need not worry about her unless she gets by my family. The tribe will protect all of you as if you were their brothers and sisters. However, you must do as they tell you so that you won't be harmed."

"I promise you that we'll do just what we're told. Is there anything that we can do to help?" Father told Mark to just do as he was told, even if it was something that went against all that he was. "All right. I will. I have my wife here that will make sure that I do what you tell me."

"Damned right, I will." They all laughed, and it was her that asked for the locks to be changed on the business that they had purchased.

"Is that important? I mean, I'll do it, of course, but is something going on?" Willow stood up and then sat down. When she smiled at Amelia, she thanked her for being so fast. "What was her plans? I'm sure that it's something to do with Barron." Father laughed as he continued telling them of the woes of Caitlynn Royce

"No, she doesn't know that he purchased the house and business. Caitlynn is unable to get into her house, thanks to you. Also, the police are there at the business, keeping her out as she is no longer the owner. All she has right now is the clothing that she has on, two checks that are as worthless as the paper that they're written on until she can get inside a bank. It's well past time for her to get inside at this hour. The check card that isn't good for another three to five business days will not purchase her a meal, not even the kind that needs to be driven around." Willow laughed. "Oh, my. She just hit an officer and is going to jail. I don't know how long she'll be there, but you can bet that she's going to call Barron to get him to bail her out. There isn't a bond on her as she hit an officer. This is much more entertaining than I thought it would be. Thank you, my child, for letting me be entertained today."

By the time they were introduced to the Indians who would be at the house at all times, Father made his way home. He didn't walk home, as he might have done before, but just disappeared. The horses, all of them palominos were put into the barn that was just suddenly there with enough fencing to give them plenty of room. They were also going to be safe from any animals that came around as they were protected by magic. Willow couldn't have been happier than she was at this very moment.

"How about you and I go home and make love?" She looked up at him and smiled. "I don't know what that means, that beautiful smile you're giving me, but I'm going to assume that it's a yes."

"It is. But I wanted you to know that it's only been a short time, but I'm in love with you. With all my being." He kissed her briefly in her mouth and held her head to his heart. "It's a lovely sound, the beating of your heart."

"It only beats because of you and my love for you." They walked hand in hand to their home. Willow was excited to be with him and was nervous, too. She'd never had sex before being so protected by the tribe, but even with that, she knew that it was going to be more than she could ever have thought. Their love for each other was a testament to how their future would be from now on.

Chapter 5

"I need to change into something more comfortable. I feel like I've been climbing through dusty closets and kitchen cabinets. I don't know why I feel that way. I just do." He asked her why and then burst out laughing when she only snapped her fingers, and she stood before him in what could only be considered a contradiction in terms of the way she was put together.

He looked down at her pants, a pair of loose-fitting flannel lounge pants that tied at the waist, her bare feet peeking out from under the legs of them made him realize, once again, that she was forever going to keep him hoping. The design nearly made him laugh, for they were a paradox with their wearer.

They were peeps, his favorite kind of marshmallow treat—especially when they were set out for a day or two and easter baskets of all sorts of colors on a bright pink background. The top, a cheerful pink sleeveless tee shirt with a dead peep on the front, was more to her temperament. The peep, a chick that was caught in a bear trap, oozing pink blood, was what had him laughing out loud. Christ, he'd been so right about her. She was forever going to keep him on his toes for the rest of their lives together.

Her shirt was tight, and her breasts were bare beneath it. As he stared at them, they swelled and tightened against the straining soft fabric. Her nipples puckered and pushed hard against the material. His breath caught, and his heart slammed against his chest. It was then that he was glad that he was an immortal. She was surely going to kill him where he stood.

When he looked at her face, he finally saw his own need and wants staring back at him. Taking in a deep breath, he could smell her need, almost feel her pussy weeping for only home.

"Come to me, Willow, now come to me. I find that if I don't have you soon, I'm going to come with not even touching your lovely body. Christ, I love you so very much." She pointed out to him that they were still in the kitchen, and he said he didn't care. "I want you right now. Please?"

She didn't hesitate but launched herself into his arms, wrapping her body around his, legs at his hips, and arms around his neck. He caught her to him and turned to press her against the closest hard surface he could find, which happened to be the refrigerator, as he took her mouth in a consuming kiss. Even for as hot as it was, he still couldn't get enough of her.

The cool, hard surface of the fridge at her back was in direct contrast to the hard heat of his body pressed to hers. He could feel that when he touched her. When he cupped her flannel-covered ass and pulled her heat closer to him, Willow threw back her head and cried loudly, giving him full access to her throat and the pulse that pounded there.

He wanted to mark her as his, but he needed to allow his bear to have his fill of her as well. As soon as he felt his teeth shift in his mouth, he licked her pulse and bit down on her tender throat, and suckled hard of her blood.

"I want you, Willow, right now. I need to be inside of you." Nodding then shaking her head, he knew just how she felt. "I love you."

He didn't wait for a reply but began working the material down her bottom so he could stroke the warm flesh it covered. Sitting her on the counter and stepping back, he yanked the pants from her and tossed them behind him just as he stepped between her legs. Reaching down, he pulled her shirt free of her body as well.

Saddened by the fact that he'd never see her wearing it again. Before it touched the table where he had tossed it, he had her nipple deep inside of his mouth, suckling it hard, his hands cupping her now bear ass once again.

She bowed into him, pressing her breast deeper into him so that he could feel the hardened tips against his own. She then tightened her legs around his hips. The thong she had on was no match for their need for each other because suddenly, they were just two scraps of lacy silk on the floor beside the peep pj's. His shirt and tie went next and suffered the same treatment as her underwear, but her hands were touching his skin, his bare, hot skin, and neither cared about the clothing anymore.

"Barron, please, upstairs. The bed is upstairs." She whispered in his ear and bit his lobe before moving closer to his neck and the muscles there. If she bit him now, which he needed more than anything, he nearly passed out waiting for her to bite him so that he could come hard. He didn't even care if he was inside of her right now.

"We'll ever make it. Now, Baby, I need you now." He stepped back again, and his knees nearly buckled at the naked woman before him.

Her small but full breasts were lifting up and down because she was panting so hard, her nipples red and swollen from his mouth had him begging for more. Her pussy was soaked, her juices shining on the curls that just covered the nether lips he so desperately wanted to fuck and taste at the same time.

"Christ, I want you."

He pushed her back against the cabinets and pulled her hips closer to the edge. He ran his finger along her heat from the bottom just to the clit that was just visible beneath the curls. He teased her with a flick of his finger before pushing into her core.

Willow nearly came off the counter, her hiss of approval driving him to deepen his assault. He watched her as he fucked her with his finger, soon adding a second, then a third, into her. She rode him, undulating her hips with each in and out movement of his fingers. Leaning in, he took her breast into his mouth again, scraping his teeth across her nipples one at a time while she got used to him invading her. Drawing a tiny bead of blood to the tip by nipping her just a little too hard, Barron drank greedily from the hard peak.

With his free hand, he pulled the snap off his dress pants and jerked the zipper down. His thick, hard cock immediately filled his hand, a tiny pearl of cum oozing from the dark crown as he fisted it up and down in time with the movements of his fingers inside of her.

When he was close, feeling the tingle of impending climax running up his spine and straight to his balls, he pulled his fingers from her reluctantly and took her mouth with his own. Her moan ripped through him, nearly making his come all over her.

"I'm large, baby, I'm sorry, but it's going to hurt you. If you want me to, we'll...Christ, I can't believe I'm saying this, but we'll stop. We will Willow; do you want me to stop?"

"I've never, I mean, I don't know. Take me, please, Barron. I want you inside of me now." She wrapped her arms around his shoulders, her body taunt with need, and he could tell a little fear. "Do it. Take me now."

Putting action to words, she tightened her legs around him once again and surged forward just as he entered her, breaking through her hymen with a hard push. She screamed with the pain as he took her virginity. He felt horrible for making her hurt and happier than he'd ever been in his life that she had waited for him to have her heart and body.

Barron stopped, his body frozen inside of hers. He could feel her body adjusting to his, pulling and tightening around his shaft. He wanted to move deeper, to empty himself in her, but he also knew that he'd hurt her more if he tried to move just now.

He kissed her gently on the mouth and kissed away her tears as they fell along her cheeks. All the while, he was touching her, murmuring things to her, soothing her, holding her as he would a small child who had a hurt. His mind was frozen. He could no more tell himself what he'd said to her than the day of the week.

"Oh baby, I'm so sorry. I didn't...well, I did mean to. I just...as soon as you are ready, I'll pull away, honey. Then a bath, I'll run you a tub full of hot water...Oh god, Willow, don't move like that...Oh yes, no, don't...Willow, please."

She started moving, to move away, he was sure, but as soon as the friction of his cock moved against her clit, she moaned, and he didn't think it was from pain. He held still, waiting for her to make the next move.

Willow tentatively moved forward against him. He, too, moved, drawing a deep moan from her. His movements were slow and measured. He didn't want to hurt her, but he could feel her need building back up with every stroke of his cock.

"Oh, my god, Barron, please. Oh, please don't stop." He knew he wouldn't be able to now, not with her legs tight around him and her pussy walls milking him.

Cupping her ass, he picked her up, and holding her tight against him, he pressed her against the fridge again, using it for leverage. Their rhythm grew frantic, their moans deeper, more demanding. When he felt her tongue trace the vein down his neck, he knew he was lost. He began to ride her harder as he searched for the vein in her throat. Licking her rapidly beating pulse, knew his own was pounding as hard as hers.

He bit her then and drew a deep pull of her into him, his own blood pouring into her mouth as she had bit him, too. Their mutual climaxes roared through them. Barron didn't stop his movement but slowed as he held her closer to him, and when she came again, sobbing his name over and over, he came hard, pouring himself deep into her.

Barron leaned his face against the cool refrigerator and tried to calm his pounding heart. He was panting hard as hell, his lungs burning as if he couldn't catch his breath. At this moment, he knew that he could die willingly and be a happy man. He held Willow to his body, his cock, still semi-hard inside of her. He straightened enough to look at her. The sated look on her face took his breath away.

"Are you all right, Love?" When she didn't answer right away, Barron turned and sat her on the counter again. "Willow?"

"I'm fine. No, I'm not fine. I'm amazed, overwhelmed, relaxed, happy, and wowed. I don't know if I'm making any sense." She snuggled her face closer to his neck, licking the droplets of blood she had missed in the bonding process. She looked up at him when he growled at her.

"You keep that up, and we will never leave this kitchen. I think you should have that bath. You're going to be sore if you aren't already." He didn't put her down but carried her still wrapped around him up to where she had pointed out which bedroom they'd be using from now on. As a couple. A mated couple. The taps were on, and the tub was filling before they got to the stairs. He didn't know which of them had used the magic to do that, but he was thrilled beyond words that the tub and the water were the perfect tempter when he got there.

As they were both naked, he stepped into the tub and settled them both into the water. Turning her around so that her back was against his chest, he began washing her with the large sea sponge that was sitting along the edge. There were candles all along the wall of the enclosure on little shelves. With a thought, he lit them for her, their scent wafting around the room. He ran the sponge up and down her arm as he held her, not really wanting to wash her so much as to touch her. And that was something he planned on doing every day, every minute, for the rest of his life.

"Now, what do we do? I mean, after we take a bath and hopefully not wake in the morning too sore." He told her that he didn't care now if the world came crashing down. He was content. "Behave. We can't just have sex all the time. We'll die of starvation. Speaking of which, I'm starving."

A small stool laden with fruits and vegetables appeared by the tub. She told him that she was set to go on a pony run with her family tomorrow that she'd nearly forgotten about. When he asked her what that meant for the tribe, she told him as if it were no big deal. To her, it might not be, but to him, it sounded like something that he'd enjoy.

"We have been scouting ponies and wild horses for the last few months. A couple of weeks ago, Running Water found a large haram that he has been keeping close to the place where we're staying. After we gather as many as we can— usually about two hundred of them- the park services pay us for each of them, and then they sell them to places around. It keeps the population down to a good number, and the tribe has money for things like flour and the like." He asked her how many she'd been on. "Ten. I mean, this will be my tenth ride. I'd love it if you could go, but it's dangerous. You could ride with me on—"

"I'll do whatever you need me to do without a moment's hesitation. I had no idea that the park did that." She told him it was a good way to keep the park from being too grazed.

"We don't do it every year but every three or four. It's an all-day event, and when we return with the horses, there is a huge celebration that lasts for a couple of days." He could hardly contain his excitement. "A lot of great horses have come from the Mountains here. It's like we've given birth to them when we hear about them in the paper."

They talked for a long time. Every time the water got a little chilled, he'd let a little out and then fill it again. When Willow laid her head on his chest to rest a bit, he knew when she'd fallen asleep. It was the greatest feeling in the world when someone trusted you enough to sleep without fear on your heart.

~*~

Willow was up before Barron the day after the ride. It had been a wonderful and successful day. They had managed to get the two hundred horses that were requested, plus enough extras that her people could train and sell off to other shifters. She'd even gotten a little too much sun but was always careful of that.

Twice, they ran into hikers, one group on motorbikes, which was strictly forbidden in the park, that were well off the paths. Barron only had to tell the office where they were, and they were run off. The very fact that they had guns and rifles and were in the path of the family and the ponies made her think that they were going to try and steal them from the tribe. She had no idea how that was going to work, but they didn't get them, and that was all the better for them.

Making her way to Maddy's home, she had some things that her father had wanted to give the young woman. It wasn't much, not in the way of giving, but she was so happy to get the few strips of leather along with some stones with holes in them that Maddy said the kids would love to work on projects with so they could have some fun. She was nearly to the front door to leave Maddy's home when she saw Thad and a shadow of a bigger boy that she'd never seen before.

It had been a very long time since she'd seen shadows of the dead. Normally, they would only appear to her if they were from her tribe or they'd had a horrific death. The closer she got to the children, the more she realized that this young man was not just a part of one of the tribes in the mountains, but he also had killed in a violent way. It looked, too, as if he'd been in the water for a while.

As she drew shadows around her so that she could listen, she called to Maddy to have her join her, not only to not be seen but to listen in as well. Whatever was going on, she thought for sure that it was something that neither of the boys wanted to be a part of but had somehow gotten trapped in a way that was going to get poor Thad and his sisters hurt. If they weren't all ready.

"John, I'm sorry about what happened to you. I am, but since people can't see you, it's going to be hard for you to get some help from us. Will you go back to the barn and keep an eye on my sisters? I promise you with all of my heart that I'll make sure that your body is found so that your parents know. I don't even care if they don't believe me, and I get a big beating for them thinking that I'm lying. I'll find you if it takes me all my life." Thad swore on his mother's heart that he'd find him for sure. "I wish I had known you before you were hurt this bad. Her pushing you over the waterfall, that wasn't nice at all, and it hurts my heart to think that she'd been making you suffer like she did. I'll find you on account of you saving me and my sisters when you did by telling us the rules of the mountain and water. Like I said, I know some people who might be able to talk to you better than I can. I know a lot of magical people, I promise you."

"That woman, she sure is loco, Thad. Her saying those things about you and your sisters is just not right. Like her saying she can feel every little bitty bug that comes in out of the rain, and it being your fault that she has to hide out in the caves. I love staying in the caves when the weather is really hard. Besides, it's raining on them too and they don't like it no more than she does. But please find my body for my mother mostly. Dad will hurt too that I can't be buried, but you make sure that you tell them that I loved them forever and will be watching over them in the great tribe in the sky."

"I will." Thad didn't see her when he looked around but it wouldn't have surprised her one bit if he had. The child and his sisters were brilliantly gifted, and they used parts of their minds that even she hadn't tapped into yet. Right then, she decided to contact Barron. He'd been feeling sorry for himself long enough, she thought with a small smile.

"We might have an issue." Barron told her just to roll him over the hill and leave him to die. He couldn't move, that every part of his body hurt like he'd been riding a horse for twelve hours, and he'd even hurt his balls. *"Goofy. I thought it was a blast. Father said you did very well for a greenhorn. But this is important. There are your people hiding in the barn. I don't know all the ins and outs, but you can bet I will before the end of the day."*

"I'm on my way. Where are they?" She told him that Maddy was with her and that it was Thad and a boy named John, who had died, and Thad's sisters. *"Should I just happen upon them while coming to find you? Tell me what to do, and I'll help all I can."*

"Do you know any faeries?" Whatever he'd been about to say, he stopped and didn't say a

word. *"I thought not. They're very secretive and don't tell people that they're around. Strawberry is the one in charge of those that are with — "*

"I'm right behind you. I'm assuming since you can see her, she's with you." Nodding when Barron sat down next to her, she put out her hand. *"I don't see anything. Just...I don't see Strawberry or a strawberry. Just tell me what it is you need me to do. You know that I'd die for you."*

Talking to Strawberry, one of her dearest friends, Willow asked Barron to listen to what the boys were saying. Willow knew whatever was going on it was a trap from Caitlynn, the crazy bitch. Why? Who knew? But it would be to capture someone — Barron's name jumped to the front of the line on the who. Also, Willow didn't know, but she'd bet anything that neither boy had gotten themselves into this predicament on their own. Maddy came back to sit with them after getting a few weapons of her own, and it was John, the little boy she barely knew, who sat down beside Maddy. Thad looked directly at them and said he was powerful, sorry.

"For what?" They didn't have time for this, not with the other children's health in the balance, but she could see the look on Thad's face and knew that he had taken on this problem to his own tiny showers. "Do you mean talking to a shadow warrior? Or perhaps the promise you made him to find his body? Either one of those will have my people calling you a hero, not someone who should be doubting themselves. You came here to get help. Thad even had you not made those promises to John here, everyone would still consider you to be one of the greatest men they know. For one so young, knowing that you needed help is a lesson that grownups still haven't learned. It's a hard thing to ask for help. You're a brave young man. It couldn't have been easy for you to have left your sisters wherever they are. They're all right, aren't they?"

"Yes, ma'am, when I left, they were. Belle is hiding in case that crazy woman comes and tries to take Maria from her. She'll knock her off the high level if she does that. I wasn't sure how to get back here, but John here, he appeared and showed me how to get back to this mountainside." Thad looked at John, who, if she remembered, was about to be sixteen. "We were looking for small things in the water. Lots of pennies that people put in the water to bring them luck. John said that it was lucky for him because sometimes he had enough money to buy something for his momma when she was down. Now he can't do that anymore."

"No. I'm terribly sorry, but we'll help her out by telling her how brave he was when he was needed. How he brought you here to get help. Not every person would have been able to do that to help people he doesn't know." She turned to John, holding onto Barron's hand while she did. "I will be indebted to you for the rest of my life, John. You know that I'm an honorable person, don't you? I will help provide for your mother, too, for the rest of her life."

It was when she went to hug the young man that she hurt the most. A senseless death all because of some crazy woman that didn't get what she wanted. Well, Willow thought, she'd messed with the wrong tribe this time. There was going to be a reckoning the likes of nothing she'd ever seen before.

Reaching out beyond where she was seated, having sat in the dirt to have the earth help with her search, she found young John just where Thad told him he was. Broken and dead at the bottom of the falls that ran along the mountain year-round, it was so swift and wide. Then, as she moved on, her mind's eye forever looked for John's relatives, and she found her father instead.

She told him everything that she knew about John and his killer. She also took the time to tell him of his shadow body and how he'd helped the Cross bears' children before he left this world to the tribe in the sky. There would be much sorrow tonight and celebration. John's parents would be honored, and his story told for many generations to come.

"Thad, they're going to get John now. His parents are going to be with them when they do. My father, the chief, would like to honor you as well. But we'll talk about that at some other time." He hugged her while he cried. Her heart was broken too for the loss of one so young. "You are a good boy, young man, and smart. Don't you ever let anyone tell you anything any different. You hear me?"

"Yes, ma'am. She just pushed him over the waterfall like he was nothing more than a stick. I didn't see him again after she pushed him. Is his...you know, is his body there. All together?"

She told him that he wasn't damaged that badly. "Good. I don't want his momma to see him messy. He was a nice person. I'm gonna keep the penny he gave me forever, too."

Chapter 6

Maria watched the woman as she stomped around the barn. She was surely glad that the mean person couldn't hear what was going on while she and Thad talked. She'd be so mad it just made her giggle a little. But to herself. Looking over at Belle, Maria winked at her while she hid under the straw. She'd fixed her up so that it didn't itch no more but they both had to pee really bad. That's where they'd been fixin' to go, to the bathroom, when she snatched her up by her nice neat ponytail.

"What is taking that brat so long?" They'd learned real quick that when she asked them a question, they weren't to answer her. She told him it was rhetorical. All three of them knew what that meant, but Maria didn't think that the woman did.

She said that it meant she knew what it meant, and they didn't. It was an adult word that they couldn't use. Thad told her that it meant that she didn't require information from it. That anyone could use it. That got him a good slap in the face. The woman came stomping over to where she was, and Maria made it so that she couldn't see Belle. "I asked you a question. What is taking that brat brother of yours so long?"

"How should I know? If I was with him, I'd be able to tell you, but then you'd not be able to ask me anything, so you'd still not know, I guess. You sent him to my parents' house, and it's a long walk when you only got ten year old legs, you know?" She drew back to slap her again, but Maria only glared at her. "Do you want me to make you hurt again?"

Maria couldn't physically hurt the woman. She couldn't hurt anyone really with her mind. All she could do was make them think that she'd punched them in the face or whatever. Or, in the case of this crazy loon, make her feel like Maria had kicked her in the legs a whole bunch of times.

Maria and her sister and brother had been out and about all morning this morning. They had found beautiful flowers that they were going to pick on the way home for their mom. John had told them the story about the Garden Fairy coming by the woods and planting them so that the animals could enjoy them when the snow melted. He also had warned them that the bulbs were poisonous and that they not eat them no matter how hungry they were.

They'd been tossing little bitty stones and sticks in the water to see how fast they went down. The bigger logs would get all caught up with other sticks and logs, and John, their new friend, had been going down to dislodge them. He said that it might cause the water to move in a different direction, and it might flood some animal homes down below. It made sense to them, but she still didn't like him risking his life by going down after them. Then that mean woman had come up on them and pushed him over the falls when he said he wasn't related to them but a friend. It still hurt her heart that he died so young.

They should have been paying more attention to what was going on around them, but they'd been so happy and having so much fun that they let themselves get caught. Belle had been napping in the upper level of the barn where they'd found a bunch of little kittens, so she didn't get snatched up by her hair when she and Thad did, but she'd been helping them with her mind to make the woman behave as much as she could. Maria was stronger than the other two, and then Thad. While Belle wasn't as strong with her mind, she could do enough to keep them as safe as she could.

"I found Mom and Dad." She could have wet her pants she'd been so happy to hear from Thad. *"I told them about the link and how it didn't work when we were so far away. He said that we'd have to take their blood when we got home. I did that already and that's why I can talk to you. I was never so happy in all my life. They're getting people gathered up to get you two. It's working now, so Mom said it might have been nerves that made it not work for us. Are you and Belle all right? I should have asked that first. Sorry."*

"Belle is still hiding. I'm glad. She'd be building up a storm of tears if that crazy woman had hit her like she did us. Are they coming to get us?" Thad told her that they were gonna use her plan. *"Good. It's a good plan, you said. That way, we won't have to be looking over our shoulders all the time about this nutball coming for us."*

"I talked to Mom about her. She said that she only wants Uncle Barron. She wants him to marry her so that she can be rich and don't have to work. I'm going to work no matter how much money I got. Mom told me that it builds character."

Maria knew the real reason that the woman, Caitlynn, wanted to marry Uncle Barron, and it had very little to do with him having money. She wanted to show off the marriage stuff that he got her to be married. The ring and the big limo. Caitlynn didn't really want to be married. She wanted all the stuff that went with it. Big everything. Party. Wedding dress. Big jewelry. That Maria didn't understand why anyone would want a big diamond ring. She had a pretend one, and it was forever falling off her hand. But then she didn't much care for boys but her family ones.

"Honey, how are you doing?" Maria had to fight really hard not to beg her Dad to come and get her when he spoke to her. She told him how she was hiding Belle and that they were waiting for them to come get them. Also that her leg was broken in two pieces. *"I'm so sorry, love. There will be someone there when we find you who will make sure*

you get good care. Your parents are coming too. We're working on that now. Aunt Amelia is going to come for you and Belle. She's going to just pop in there and pop back out with you so that you'll know when we arrive. Just stay where you are and we'll take care of you getting out of the barn. All right?"

"Yes, but I have to tell you, Dad, that crazy woman had all kinds of guns and knives. She wants to make it so that Uncle Barron marries her. That boy that was with us, his name is John, she's gone and killed him like he wasn't a person or anything. I guess Thad told you all about that. My goodness, Dad, my heart hurts bad for him and his momma right now."

"We have known about him, sweetie. He'll be picked up by his people and taken care of in their own way. Don't you worry about a thing, honey. We'll be there soon. She beat you guys up pretty badly, didn't she?" Maria told him that she'd knocked them down a long hill and into the water until they thought they were going to die. *"You're getting help now. As soon as Amelia gets there, don't say a word but take her hand into yours. But you have to warn me when Caitlynn has her back to you so that she doesn't hurt the three of you."* She asked if her mom and brother would be there. *"Yes. They're waiting right*

here, baby. We'll all be coming in the second chopper so they can get help to you guys before we pick you up and squeeze the love out of you."

She told Belle to get ready to stand up. Maria was glad that she'd said that before Aunt Amelia came. Belle had cramps in her legs for laying for so long. Telling them that Belle was going to need help had her daddy cursing. He didn't do it very much, but he surely did today. Maria just told Aunt Amelia to do the popping thing to get Belle, then come back for her. It was done in seconds.

Aunt Amelia not only popped in to get Belle, but she kissed them both on the cheeks and carried her sister out and came back for her all without the crazy woman ever knowing. She'd never been so happy to see her little brother as she was then. Hugging them all, including her aunts and uncles, Maria cried, big girl tears Jamie called them when they were all safe. Now they had to get the crazy woman and poor John.

As soon as she was a bit away from the barn, Maria watched as the men dressed all in green with guns and knives on them made their way, sneaky-like, toward the barn. Stopping one of them, a real nice man that called her Miss and everything, she told him to be extra careful that the crazy woman had several guns and a bag of knives. He then asked her if she'd noticed her having any kind of bombs.

"Gee whiz, Mister, I didn't even think of that. But she just has guns and knives. Do you think that a bomb—you know, never mind. I don't want to know if you know how to disable a bomb or not. In my head, I'm going to tell you that you can. I'm scared enough about that crazy bat." He laughed and then mussed her hair. "Do you know if anyone is going to get me a drink or something? I'm very thirsty." He handed her his unopened bottle and made his way down the hill more. She was going to write him a thank you note. Her mom told her that was the proper way and the nicest way to thank someone.

~*~

Caitlynn tossed the straw or hay, whatever the hell it was everywhere, trying to find where that damned girl was hiding. She was her ticket to getting Barron. She was going to be the one who found the kids, brought them to safety, and then be the hero. Who didn't love a hero? Everyone would love her and treat her as the best thing since sliced watermelon. Her grandda used to say that to her all the time, Caitlynn just remembered.

The kids had been tossing sticks, not too many of them, over the falls to have a race to see which one got to the bottom the fastest. It was a silly game, but it entertained them enough that she was able to sneak up behind them and hit them all over the head. The bigger boy, he was a bit harder to get to go down. After telling her that he was going to find their parents, she shoved him off the top of the falls and threatened the other two – or three. It seemed to her there were three little kids there. Not that it mattered. She wasn't going to go out and look for another kid for them when she thought that two was two too many. Now they were all missing, and she didn't know how the hell that had happened.

So far, all they had done was complain and bitch about everything. The stuff they were sitting on was too itchy. They had to pee. Didn't she bring them any snacks? The one with the broken leg was the noisiest. All she did was cry that Caitlynn had broken her leg and that her daddy and mommy were going to be so mad at her. She hated it when they whispered, too. Calling her what she thought was Crazy Caitlynn. Even watching them, she couldn't see them saying it, but it was circling around in her head like a mantra all the fucking time. Crazy Caitlynn, over and over.

The pee-whining one got on her nerves the most. How many times did a kid have to pee in one day, for Christ's sake? It wasn't like she was letting them get into the water to get a drink or anything. Not even when the water wasn't raging by them she made them stay back. She was going to have the two kids even if she had to listen to their shit for the rest of the day.

Now the damned little boy was gone—she'd sent him to find a police officer or whatever they were called around here and bring them here. She knew that she was taking a chance in him telling his version of what happened and not what she told him to tell them, but she'd take care of that with a couple of wallops to the head.

He was to bring the officer, just one of them, to come and find them because and she had to make sure he remembered how to say it four times that she'd found the Cross children, that she was their hero. Also, Caitlynn told him that he'd better never mention the other boy, or she'd come after him and his family in the middle of the night and cut all their throats.

There were police everywhere in the forest around the only fucking barn that she'd been staying in since she'd found it. There were drones, too, a lot of them zooming around like it was an international airport, and they had to get into the sky all at the same time. Helicopters too. Christ, those things were loud. But not one of them landed to help her get rid of these damned kids.

Of course, she'd not found them yet but had been trying to find a place to pee when she came upon them playing with some other kid that she had to get rid of. He was strong, and when she found out he wasn't related to the Cross kids, she just pushed him over the waterfall where they'd been playing. Christ, both were a pain in the fucking ass if you asked her. It didn't matter if they were big or little. They were a pain in the flipping ass. However, something did bother her just enough to make her think that she was going mad.

She would have sworn there were three of them kids after tossing the extra one off the hill. But neither of the two would tell her any different, and that pissed her off enough to have had to her break the leg of the little girl. That was a stupid mistake she made. She knew that when she had to carry the brat everywhere. If she'd killed her, that would have lightened her load and only given her one to keep track of. Then Barron, the slimy bastard wouldn't take to her killing off one of his brothers' kids. But she surely was tempted all the time.

Climbing down the ladder to get to the main section of the barn, Caitlynn wondered again why barns weren't equipped with elevators or even stairs. How on earth did they get the pigs and cows up to the top to eat the grass, straw, whatever it was? She'd seen a horse or two while hiding out. They would have been impossible for five men to carry up the barn ladder, not to mention they were so narrow she barely could get up there without carrying a damned thing.

Perhaps that was why horses were forever out in the grassy areas. Because they were just too big to carry up those stairs. But still, she thought, there wasn't any possible way for a person to be able to climb up them with anything but using both your hands. And climbing down was worse.

How was one supposed to see where they were putting their feet as they got down to the next one?

Coming out of the other half of the barn — that was another thing that confused the hell out of her. Why did a barn need two big doors, wide enough to pass your car through, when they could just have one opening and not have to worry about the cold or weather getting to the animals and hay straw stuff? Also, who knew which was the front or the back as they both had large openings there to get confused over. Christ, no wonder farmers were at the bottom of the line of smart people. They couldn't even build a simple structure to keep their animals in. She would hate to see what their homes looked like.

As she turned while trying to brush a thousand years of dust and shit off her to look presentable, a shadow passed over her, and it took her a moment in the blinding sun to realize who it was. The man standing there was the one man that she wanted above all others. She started toward him and stopped when he put up his hand. Still unable to look at his face with the glare Caitlynn might give that brat nephew of his a hug if he were here now.

Men stood up behind him. It looked as if they had guns. All of them pointed in her direction, but more than likely, it was at the kids. She couldn't find fault with them, the kids had been a pain in the ass, and she'd not go near them either for whatever germs they might have. Then the sun was washed out, and she could see him perfectly. Taking another step toward him, she nearly sobbed she was so thrilled.

"Barron. Oh, love, how I've missed you." When he backed up, too far for her to touch him, she noticed that there was an Indian standing next to him. Caitlynn wasn't positive that she was using the right term for the man, but he certainly looked like the Indians of the old west movies she'd watched with her grandda when he'd been alive. "What's going on? I see that you've found the kid. I sent him for you when I knew I couldn't find my way back with the two of them. One of them has a broken leg. You have no idea how hard it's been for me to keep them safe until I found you."

"Is that the story that you're going to stick to, Caitlynn? Or do you want a few minutes to come up with something else? Before I let you do that, I'd like for you to meet Chief Grey Wolf Ironhorse.

His boy has been missing since early this morning, and we have a story about you like my nephew does. They said that you beat them. Then, when you found out that young John wasn't a Cross, you pushed him over the waterways and killed him. I believe them over anything you might say because you're a liar since you were a child. Isn't that right?"

"I haven't any idea what you're talking about. Kids are natural-born liars, all of them. I think that was something that you brought up when you and I talked about not having children. Remember that. It was right after you asked me to marry you." He said that he was already married. "I'm sorry, what?" She laughed, looking around to see if anyone else thought it was funny. "You can't be married, Barron. You and I have plans to wed. Remember? It was going to be a huge wedding with all kinds of important guests. You were going to be showing me off, you told me. You have to remember that. It's not that long ago."

"We never discussed marrying in any capacity, Caitlynn. I remember a conversation that you and I had about me telling you that I didn't love you. That you and I would never have children as we weren't mates. I never asked you—"

"You did say that to me. That we couldn't have any children. Yes, I remember that. It was when you asked me to marry you. You're getting things all messed up in your head, Barron. You have to marry me. You have no idea…that's who that was. I remember him now. The man that I sold my house and business to was…it was the president of the United States. I did meet him in the restaurant, and you told him that we were going to get married then. He offered us the White House. Remember?" Barron just shook his head. "Well, whatever. You're going to marry me, and we'll be the happiest…my goodness, we can have the president in our home. Wait…I don't have a home. I sold it to him. Or someone with him. Who was that?" Barron said that his name had been David Rugby, an FBI agent was the second man, but she'd sold it all to him. "I don't know if that's true or not, but he can come to the wedding too. He cleans up very well, don't you think?

"You're going to be arrested and then—" Caitlynn stopped talking when he literally shoved her out of the way when she heard someone call him Uncle Barron. There were two fucking girls up in the barn. She was right. The little fuckers were going to pay and pay big for that. "You little shits."

Slapping them both, Caitlynn heard the sharp inhalation of breath before she started on the girls.

"I told you there were three of you brats. I was right. See if I don't punish you bad, you little fuckers. All you've done is made my life a living hell since I found you playing with that brat. And here you both are standing there like you've been out to a party." One of them mentioned that she'd broken her leg. "You're just lucky that I was trying to impress your uncle with what a great person I am, or I would have strangled you and left you for the animals to eat. Christ, I hate you kids. All kids are nothing but little fuckers, and I hope you both die for what you did to me."

It was then that she realized what she'd been saying. The silence around her was deafening, turning slowly, she smiled at Barron as he held the one with the broken leg in his arms. The other little fucker was clinging to his leg like he was some kind of hero. Well, she was the hero, not him, damn it. He was going to marry her too, by god.

"She told Becky if she cried anymore that she was going to chop her tongue out and feed it to the fish. Her, too, with a rock tied around her leg." Caitlynn told her to shut her mouth. "I will not. Did Thad find you guys? He sure is hurt, almost like when that man would take us from Mom. Uncle Barron, you're squeezing Belle too tight right now."

"I'm sorry, honey." He loosened his grip on the kid and knelt down at the other girl's level. "Why don't you climb up on my back and shoulders, honey? That way, I can take you both out of here. I don't want you around her any more than you want to be. All right. Your parents are on their way in the next chopper."

She didn't speak to anyone, but she did follow Barron towards the helicopter when it landed. The kid in his arms was taken from him as soon as the blades stopped rotating so fast, and she reached for the one on his back. As soon as she touched the little girl, it was like she was tangling with a wild animal. And no one seemed to care either that she was getting the shit knocked out of her.

When the little girl was finally lifted off her,

it had to have been at least twenty minutes before anyone else moved. Caitlynn laid on the ground without moving. She knew her face was bloodied and that there would be scars all over her. The blood that was running down her forehead was getting into her eyes and mouth. Wiping it off and looking at the kid, she saw too that she'd pulled out hanks of hair, big wads of it that would take forever to grow back.

"Look what you've done to me." She laughed and lunged at her again. Lucky for...well, she didn't know if it was lucky for her or the kid, but she was glad that Barron had still had a tight hold on her. "You little monster. You're going to pay for this. I don't care if they put you in kiddy prison for the rest of your life, either."

One of the medics came to where Barron and the brat were. He checked her out, acting like she'd been somewhat of a savior who had killed the ugly beast. While Barron held onto the child, the medic told them what he was going to be doing with each step he took with the child. When the handful of hair was dislodged from her clenched fingers, it was put into a baggie with the word evidence written on it.

"See that, girly? They're going to bring that to the courtroom to show as evidence that you tore out my hair." The child said that she wished she'd been able to snatch her bald. Sitting up and going after her one more time, Caitlynn was knocked back, and a boot was put on her chest. "What are you doing? That little monster is the one that attacked me. I was just trying to help her get to the ambulance thing."

"I think she's showing us how much she hates you, Caitlynn. Does she have good reason to?" Caitlynn didn't answer Barron but let it go for now. She'd just decided that she was going to have herself and Barron move to another part of the world. In fact, with his money, she was going to go to the moon with him. That way, she'd have him...no, no, that'd not work. No one would be there to admire her with Barron if she did that." Her mind was working hard, and it took her some time to realize that someone was saying her name.

Turning to look at the men behind her, she put on her best smile. She never got smart with people wearing guns, nor did she ever try to run from them. That was a good way to get yourself shot up. Asking the first man standing there if she could help him, she tried not to notice that all the other men had their guns pointed directly at her head.

"I don't know what is going on here, but I saved these children, and I won't have you saying otherwise." No one moved and she stomped her foot at them. "Do you have any idea how much money my future husband has? If you don't lower those guns, I'm going to make sure that we have all your money and then have you put into prison for the rest of your lives." She looked at Barron. "Well? Are you going to do anything about this?"

"I think that they're doing a splendid job with what they're doing right now." She said that they were pointing their guns at her. "Yes, and you're just lucky that I'm not holding a gun on you right now. I'd be willing to go to prison for the rest of my life and blow your head off for what you've done to my family."

"I haven't any idea what you're talking about." She was pissed off that he didn't clarify what he was talking about. "Barron, you can't let a little thing like this ruin what we had, can you? I mean, I have...no, we've made plans, and you're going to stick to them."

"Nope." She hated that word and hated it even more when it was used when talking to her. "I don't want anything to do with you. As I've said to you several times now, I don't love you. I never have. I am married to a wonderful woman who doesn't manipulate everything that I say around to benefit her. So, as far as I'm concerned, you can rot in hell for the rest of your days. I have only hatred toward you and want nothing more to do with you."

When the helicopter took off, a third one was landing. The kids were all gone, as well as what she assumed was their mother. That was when she realized that she was going to lose it all if she didn't think of something fast. But before she could come up with a plan, she was being handcuffed and shackled around her legs. Even if she wanted to run, there wasn't any way that she'd get all that far before they'd catch her. Looking around for Barron, she noticed that he was talking to someone she'd not noticed before. A very beautiful woman that looked perfect next to him. However, when they kissed, like they were lovers, Caitlynn lost control and lunged at them.

She'd forgotten that she was chained up,

and when she hit the ground, it was almost as if water sprouted all around her, and she was tossed around in water and rocks. As soon as her head was above the water, she'd hit something else, and under she'd go again.

Getting glimpses of people putting out their hands to grab her, she felt herself tumble over and over the big rocks. As suddenly as she felt like she was floating in the air, with water flowing quickly around her, she was under again. Christ, this wasn't the way she wanted to get out of going to prison.

Every time she felt the air, not water, around her face, she tried to grab as much air as she could. But all she got was water in her face, and on some level, she knew that she was going to be disfigured for the rest of her life when she got out of this mess.

Seeing a large rock in front of her, she tried grabbing it with her chained hands just as the rock disappeared. Caitlynn hurt everywhere on her body. She was sure she had broken a lot of bones. Going under again, she was tangled up on some logs that had long since been buried in the water and mud beneath it. Her head, below the surface of the water, made her think that perhaps she was going to die. Christ, she wasn't ever going to see all her plans come to fruition if she became fishy food.

Chapter 7

"Yes, sir. Everyone there tried to save her, but the rapids with the spring fall coming along made the water deeper and quicker than usual. One of the men who was trying to save her lost his life when he slipped into the fast-moving water and drowned before we could find him." Barron wanted to stretch his neck and let go of the pressure that was building up behind his eyes. "We were able to recover both bodies, that of the ranger and Ms. Royce. We're awaiting word from the FBI to figure out if she has any family left that wants to claim her body. Ranger Cauldwell's family is going to have him cremated as soon as the body is released to them. I'm to understand that there had been a fund set up for his family as well. He and his wife had just had their first child a few weeks prior to this incident."

Incident? What a mundane word to call the tragic death of three people. There had been no reason for any of the deaths but the greed and stupidity of one woman. He had to ask the man in charge of this inquiry what he'd said.

"I'm sorry, young man. I bet you'd rather be anywhere but here with us at this time. I'm to understand that the tribe has taken care of their own family member." He told him that he was the brother of his wife. "Yes, let me offer you both congratulations as well as condolences, and I have just one more question for you before we finish this up. Do you have any reason to believe that Ms. Royce had anything to do with the deaths of her parents? It is said around town where she was from that she is responsible for the deaths of a great many children."

Caitlynn could, and he hoped that she would rot in hell for all that she'd done, but it wouldn't help anyone to exhume the bodies of her parents and he told the man that.

"I think, and this is just me thinking out loud, that she should be charged with every unexplained death of anyone in that little town she was from. You'd ask why, and I would as well. But if she's charged with their murders, dead or not, it will, hopefully, give closure to a great many parents who lost their children to her not getting what she wanted." He thought that was an excellent idea. "Thank you, sir. I'm sure you would have come up with it sooner or later. It would, for me, as well give some people a chance to blame someone else for the deaths of their children rather than thinking that they'd failed them in some way."

"Yes, most excellent. That's what we're going to do then." When the men at the table stood up, he did as well. He just wanted to go home, make love to his wife, and sleep for about a thousand years. "Ranger Cross, I do hope that in the future, we can depend on you for help on matters like this. Finding those bodies was a good thing, and we, as part of the National Park Service can't thank you enough for all that you and your family have done for this park and others like it. Thank you again."

After shaking their hands, he made his way out of the building. It was warming up down here in the town, but the mountains where he lived were still cold. Just the way that he liked it. As he went to get into his truck, he saw Willow leaning against it and couldn't have been happier. After kissing her, he decided that he was suddenly starving. She had packed them a picnic lunch and they were going to find a nice place in the park that wasn't too busy this time of year and have a good time.

"My father is ready to have the ceremony for John. He wants us both to be there. I hope you don't mind, but I told him that we would and that we'd be happy to help with whatever they needed." He told her that was an excellent idea. "Thanks. How did things go in the meeting? I'm assuming since you weren't arrested, everything is cleared up now."

"Yes. They're going to take care that the ranger's wife and child get his insurance money. And they also said that as a park they'd contribute to the fund that the bank is having for them. We donated a bit of money to it, as well as the rest of my family." She nodded and handed him a thick roast beef sandwich.

He also told her about what he said about blaming Caitlynn for the other murders in their town and what they were going to do about them. She told him that was something that she wanted to talk to him about and was glad that someone was going to help those other families. He asked her what she'd been doing today.

"After taking my second shower after you mussed me all up, I went to talk to the kids. They're the watchers of the faeries. I did ask you once before if you knew about them, the faeries, I mean, and we got sidetracked. Strawberry wants to speak to you." Before he could ask her about that, she dumped a small leather bag of small items on the blanket they were using. "Your grandmother was the watcher before Gibb and his family were watchers. No one knows about them but your family. If you figure out how to see them, you'll notice them more and more just flittering about all the time. But you have to believe that they're real in order to do that."

He picked up a small shell no bigger than the tip of his smallest finger. He asked her why she was collecting things like this when she explained what his grandmother did. How she would find them things and put them in a tin so that they could come and go when they wanted something she'd found.

"The small tin that sat in the window over

the sink. The window was open all the time, I remember now. Even in the winter months. She never explained anything else about it just that we were never to shut the window." Willow said that was right. "What's happening now that my grannie is gone?"

"Gibbs family is taking over her job. The children will gather things that they find, even if you'd think it was too large for them to use, they use their magic and cut it down so that everyone that wants a part of it can have some." The things in the pile were moving around on their own, and he watched as Willow continued with her story. "Sometimes, it's only a scrap of yarn or a broken toy. She would take it apart and put it in the can. They found use for everything that was found for them."

As he continued to watch the things move on their own, he started to see things. A pair of wings that were simply floating in the air. Sparkles of bright colors were there as well. Then, when he believed that he was seeing something real, he saw the fifty or so faeries that were sorting through the things on the blanket that Willow had dumped out.

Careful of not to move too quickly, he stretched out his legs to get into the front pocket of his jeans and put the things that he'd collected too. She asked him why he'd done that.

"I don't know that they can use any of this." Just then, the small shiny bead that he'd found just this morning was picked up by one of the little persons. "The kids, they were picking up things out of the forest one afternoon when we were hunting for truffles. They were picking up little rocks and stones that were as smooth as a piece of glass. Even things that should have been put in the trash, like twisty ties in their pockets. They told me that they use them for crafting. After that day, I began picking things up and keeping them in my pocket so that I could give them to them when I saw them the next time."

One of the faeries landed on his knee and looked at him. He'd bet anything that this was Strawberry. Every part of her was red like a fresh berry, and she was wearing a top of one of the berries as a hat. Christ, she was so beautiful that he had to tell her that.

"Thank you, my lord. You are most generous with your things, too." He told her that it was his pleasure. "There are so many of us now that someone is carrying for us that we've no more room in the house of Gibb and the children. We have come to you and your lady wife to see if we might become a part of your household as well. I promise you that no harm will ever come to you and yours so long as we are there. Nor will we cause you trouble while staying with you." He looked over at Willow, and at her nod, he told Strawberry that it was fine with him. "Thank you. We will protect your home too while there, and as a gift for helping us, we'll make sure that your gardens are plentiful and beautiful."

"Thank you so much for that help." The things on the blanket were nearly gone when they decided that they'd better be getting home. When asked how he'd leave things out for them, Strawberry asked if he could just put a jar by the window, and they'd come and go as they wanted. "I do hope that you'll stop to talk to us while you're around getting things. Also, if you find that you could use more than we can find here on the mountain, you let me know, and I'll make sure you get it. Even if I have to cut something down for you to use in smaller pieces."

After packing up the things that Willow had brought to eat and letting the little people take what they wanted of the things left over, they were ready to go. It had been fun for him to cut up the leftover grapes for them. It was a treat for all of them to have some of the juicy fruits. Packing things in the truck, he found a gift wrapped box on the seat of his truck. He asked Willow about it.

"I don't know what it is. It smells like the faeries, but I don't know. He sniffed the ribbon that was on the gift and could smell the scent of fresh strawberries. Opening it up, he was happy that he'd been gifted a bag, much like Willows, to put things in while he was out. He did ask Willow what the writing was on the front of it.

"It's your name in faerie. I've never known them to do that before. Put someone's name on a pouch that they've made for someone. And I'm betting like mine, it's an endless bag, too. The magic will allow you to put all manner of things in the bag, and it will be room for anything you wish to put in it. So you can carry a great deal and not be weighed down by it. That is a very special gift, Barron. As I said, I've never known them to do something like this for a person they've only met today."

As they made their way home, he couldn't help but be touched by the gift. He'd tied it to his belt and then thought better of it. He didn't want it to get lost, so he'd have to figure out a way to make it stay on his person. Willow told him that he was to wear it around his neck and that while there, no one would see it unless he showed it to them. That's what he did, too. Put it around his neck so that he'd have it with him whenever he needed it. Getting out of the truck when they got home, he found a small geode and put it in his pouch. Smiling, they entered the house to get some work done while there.

The ceremony was this evening, and he was glad that they'd been invited. He had spent most of yesterday helping the others get ready for all the people coming. They didn't want any meat at the meal, so he'd been more than happy to ask the faeries to gather up as much fruit and other things so that they'd have enough. They were, of course, more than happy to help out.

They couldn't drive to the place where the Indians were, so they rode their ponies. He wasn't nearly as sore as he thought he'd be this time, but he did have to walk off a little bit of pulled muscles when he got there. Willow looked as if she'd been doing it all her life and more than likely had been. He knew that before the end of the summer, he'd be riding like a pro. Or he'd been confined to a wheelchair. Horseback riding wasn't anything for the faint of heart, he discovered.

~*~

"This is what I could find out about your parents." Taking the thick file from Mark, she asked him if they'd abandoned her in the park on purpose. "From what I can tell, it looks like they did it several times over their lifetime, and up until you were left, they were doing it at all the parks, suing each park for the loss of life. A couple of the kids were older than you were when they were left behind, so they were old enough to figure out how to find help. After that, they left younger ones behind. Your brother, Thomas, saw them enter the park with you when he was nineteen. He hadn't seen them since he'd been about twelve years old, so it was a miracle that he was able to recognize them at all." She asked if he tried to save her. "Yes, he did. But you had already been found by the tribe, I think, and he lost you in the park. However, he was able to prove in court that they'd been doing this for a very long time. You were presumed dead about the time you turned sixteen, and your body was never recovered. Now we know why."

She nodded, looking at the pictures that Mark had been able to find for her. They're both dead, your parents, I mean. They'd been in prison on another crime when there was a prison riot, and both of them were killed after killing a couple of guards. No one claimed their bodies, so they're buried in the prison graveyard with only a number on their headstones. You have two sisters and Thomas as family."

"Do they know about me?" Mark nodded and smiled. "You told them what happened to me, didn't you? I can't thank you enough for that. I don't know what I'd say if I had to tell them what had happened." She smiled at him.

"You're very welcome. Your name isn't Willow, as you thought. When you said that you thought that that's what your father called you, it was Wilma, not Willow. If you ask me, I think Willow suits you better. Your last name is, was Hollister." She looked over the handful of pictures, not remembering anything about the people in them. Not even when it was pointed out which person she was did she remember who any of them were. "Willow, they would love to meet you. I told them that it would be entirely up to you as you've been without them in your life for so long that you might not want to get—"

"How can I get in touch with them? I want to...I might not know them, but they do me, so I'd be honored if I was able to meet them." Mark looked over her shoulder, and she turned to look. Barron was there with some people. From the pictures, she knew that the three people in front were her brother and sisters. "Hello?"

They started out timidly in saying anything. It wasn't until Barron told them that this was his wife and that she'd been going by Willow since she'd been found. After a few seconds, tears were flowing quickly, and Thomas asked if he could have a hug. Then it was everyone hugging everyone while they spoke over each other.

Barron sat with her as they told her who everyone was. She had not just a brother and two sisters but she had nieces and nephews as well. The youngest, Wilma Jean, was only three months old but looked like her when she'd been a child, according to the pictures. After she got to hold her, she told them what had happened the day that Chief John had adopted her into his family.

"I've been brought up like a Cherokee since they found me. He's always told me that I must have only gotten lost a few hours before he found me by the water's edges as I was still clean and had a full belly. It was the first time I remember thinking that anyone had held me in their arms. I don't know why that popped into my head, but it's stuck with me ever since."

"It more than likely was the first time. They never wanted any of us, so why they continued to have us is beyond me." Willow asked her sister Sara Jane how many there had been. "So far, we've been able to find out that in addition to the four of us, there might well have been as many as eight more. All of their names come up as they'd died and nothing more. Amelia, who had been sitting quietly in the living room with them, smiled at them all. She introduced herself as the grand witch. She'd forgotten about that.

"Your parents lost custody of the four that were still living at home when Willow came up missing. Thanks to Thomas, they figured out that it was only a matter of time before they were lost, too. They, too, sadly are dead, not by any nefarious means but because of some DNA illness that didn't allow them to be healthy in their lives. The others, as you said, four of them, have grown to be adults. The oldest is in his late seventies and in poor health. He knows nothing about his family, not even the one that he was raised as their own. He has dementia. Now that I've been able to locate him, thanks to the Cross Foundation, he's in a better nursing home and getting excellent care for the rest of his life. His name is David Bing. There was a set of twins born not too long after David was born. They were separated by the State when they were infants and haven't known of each other until recently. They're going to meet each other at the end of this month. I think that I would get in touch with their attorney before then and see if you can all get together. And, of course, the foundation will help with the arrangements for that, too."

"And the last child? Do you know who or where they are?" Amelia nodded and stood up. "She's here, isn't she? I have another sister."

"You have another brother. His name is Nathaniel Waynes. Mr. Waynes is someone that this family knows very well. He is on the board of the National Park Service and has been, in his spare time, looking for Willow since he'd found out her story. He is here. Waiting to see if you'll accept him as willingly as you have the rest of the family." She stood up when the door to the library opened. "Everyone, I'd like for you to meet Nate Waynes, the last family member that has been found for the rest of you."

Hugs were given all around again. Nate was in a wheelchair and blind. Again, the DNA from their parents had plagued him with bad health, but he had parents who had enough money to find him only the best doctors when he'd been sick. Willow sat down in front of the elderly man and smiled at him. He put his hand out, and she put it on her cheek as she spoke to him.

"I met you long ago, do you remember?" He said that he did now that he knew where she'd been living. "You were giving a lecture on what dangers were in the park and that they needed to hire good people to be there for any family member who needed help. You didn't point me out, not then, but you found me later to tell me that you were still looking for my family. I hadn't any idea that my family was standing right in front of me."

"Chief John told me that he'd found you wandering around one afternoon and that he'd thought that the parents had done it. It wasn't until years later that I'd heard the stories of what my parents had done to their children before I remembered you. I've been searching for you since. My goodness, you were such a brave little thing back then. I've no doubt that you are still like that little girl."

"Yes, sir. She's the most beautiful creature ever created if you ask me." She introduced him to Barron, and the two of them talked about their dealings with the forest and being park rangers. Willow made her way out of the house and to the back deck. It was overwhelming, just a little how close she'd been to her brother while living in the park. The door opened and closed behind her, and she smiled at Father when he asked if he could join her.

"I never thought once that you'd not have plenty of people to love you, child. The old saying is true that when one door closes, something else will open so that you can get on with your life as it needs to be." She knew that he wasn't close to having it right, but she agreed with him. "My sons and wife are gone now, and I have a daughter that will be taken away from me soon."

"You have another daughter that I don't know about? Because if you think you're losing me, old man, you're sadly mistaken. I plan to have plenty of children and raise them the same way that you and the tribe did me. I don't see either of us leaving this mountain anytime too soon. And if you play your cards right, I might just name my first son after you. How does John Tennessee Roanhorse Cross sound? Or John Alamo Cross? I have to be careful not to use too many parts of your name, or I'll run out before I stop having babies. Even a little girl or two might come along with your name."

He cried and held her in his arms. His heart, forever betting so strongly, felt good pounding in her ears. Father told her that he loved her. Both in English and in his own language. She asked him what his wife's name was. She didn't think that she'd ever heard it. His laughter made her smile. It was such a strong sound that she knew whatever he had to tell her was going to make her laugh hard, too.

"Her name was Willow Buffalo Highwater. Don't you dare name any of your daughters Buffalo. They will never have a moment of peace. My goodness, I haven't thought of that in decades. She hated her name, but it was given to her by her grandmother, who was a spiteful old woman, and she's hated it since." They both laughed and decided it was time for them to join the others. She was amazed that they were all getting along so well, and when they were invited, all of them went to dinner, and the big limos that the family had made a huge impression on her father. He, more than anything in the world, was all the family that she needed. But it was wonderful to have so much family, too.

Dinner was a big success. Her brother Nate said that he had a great many pictures that he had been saving for his children, but sadly, he'd never had anyone other than his wife. She died not long ago, and Nate lived alone in DC, where he could keep an ear out for found children. He told her how he'd set up a foundation that would be used to help children be relocated with their parents, if that was the way to go. They were all leaving, with the exception of her father, at around midnight.

He took Barron and the other Cross brothers aside to speak to them once more before leaving.

The sun was coming up when Barron joined her in bed. His body was chilled, but he soon warmed up when he snuggled up to her. He told her bits and pieces of the conversation that he'd had with her father and about the tribe that he had. Exhaustion hit him hard. As soon as his head hit the pillow, she didn't think that he moved for the rest of the night. It had been a very long week this week, and she, in a way, didn't want it to end. That meant that, to her, the family that she'd married into and only just found would be doing their own things in life, and she wouldn't be able to spend all day with them.

Willow got up at her usual time, leaving Barron to rest a bit more. After getting her shower and getting dressed, she was on the way to the barn to work with the ponies when she doubled over in pain. Going to her knees, her heart and body feeling ripped from her chest, she knew that her father, the only one that she'd ever known, had let out his last breath. That he had joined his son in the heavens of the big tribe in the sky.

She was still on her knees when Maddy

found her sometime later in the morning. Telling her about her father, Maddy sat with her until the children came to find them. As she was telling them that her father had died, that he was no more, they sat on her lap, each of them hugging her tightly.

"Your father was a great man. I know you know that but when people tell me that my father is a great man, even though I know it, it sure does feel good." Willow hugged Maria tightly and thanked her for that. "The tribe has had a lot of things happen this week. So have you, Aunt Willow."

"Yes, but this will not be met with sorrow, not for long anyway, but happiness. He had a good, long life, and he is going to be with his sons and wife in the sky." Thad asked her if she knew which stars made up the tribe in the sky. "I do. And tonight, I'll point it out to you. It's a long arrow that has lots of stars for its feathers. Tonight and every night for a month, those stars will shine the brightest because they will be welcoming a wonderful person into their arms, and they'll want every other star to know it."

They sat there until Barron came out of the house. He only kissed her on the forehead for her to know that he'd figured it out as well. Soon all the Cross brothers were there and were headed to the tribe to help with the big celebration. Every tribe in the mountains would be represented tonight to pay homage to a great leader like her father was. She was telling them how she would be wearing her own happiness costume so that people would understand that she was the last of the Chief's children. Maria asked if it mattered that she wasn't like them, an Indian.

"No. I was adopted into their tribe, and I was never treated differently than a child born of the tribe. I will have to find someone to be the chief as women aren't to run the tribe, but I think that was what the men were talking about last night." She looked at Barron. "Did he ask you to take over his place in the tribe?"

"Yes. It's an honor for me to do so. With you at my side, we'll do the best we can. I just didn't think he would pass on so soon. I'm going to miss the old man." She laughed with Barron, and she told him stories of growing up with the other children. She was going to miss him forever, but having Barron with her, she knew that things would be just right.

Chapter 8

The last few days had been hectic. If she wasn't running to the tribe to settle some kind of fight, she was at the house she and Barron were building to settle on the carpet color or what shade of blue they wanted the roofing. Stopping in her tracks, she decided if she didn't take five minutes for herself, she was going to scream. Going past the house that looked nearly finished to her, Willow made her way to the fast-moving water of the mountain waterfall.

The water would be cold, it didn't mean how deep into summer they were. She was going to dive into the waters and plunge herself into the deepest part of the water and not come up for at least a full minute. She figured that would be just long enough for her to scream out her frustrations and feel better about her day. But looking down over the falls, she knew that she'd be a fool to leap right now. The spring thaw was still coming from the mountain, and she didn't want to kill herself while getting relaxed, too. She decided to find herself a smallish pond of water and swim for a bit. Hearing something deep in the woods, she saw a man off in the distance and knew that it was Barron.

Willow nearly turned around and left the tiny wooded bath area when she saw what he was doing. But found she couldn't. He was gloriously naked and standing in the only bit of sunlight shining down through the trees. Watching as he wrapped his hand around his cock and moved it up and down. She couldn't help the moan that spilled over her suddenly dry lips.

When he turned toward her, taking the needed steps that would bring them together, she wanted to reach out and stop him from gripping his cock. Willow wanted to do it, to help him release out here in the land where they both had been from.

"If you continue to stand there watching me

masturbate, I'm going to come all over you." She looked up at his face when he spoke. Tearing her eyes away from his thick full cock was the hardest thing she'd ever done. "Come here, Willow. Help me come."

She moved toward him, reaching out her hand to touch him as he took her hand and rubbed it against his shaft. Wrapping her fingers around him as he'd done and squeezed him, the grith of him was always such a pleasure to feel, especially inside of her. He jumped in her hand. When his free hand moved behind her neck and brought her close, she moaned again when she felt his mouth nip at her neck.

"Strip. Take your clothes off and let me taste you. Don't slow down, Willow. I'm so close now that I can barely contain myself. Christ, I want to fuck you with my tongue." His hands were everywhere, and her clothes were torn from her even as she felt his mouth on her breasts. The tree behind her was rough feeling. But only for a few seconds. It felt amazing to have him treat her so wonderfully and fuck her so hard. "Feed me, Willow. Feed me your nipples while I fuck your hand."

When her breast was free, she lifted it up to his mouth, and his teeth sank deep into her nipple, making her cry out. When he turned her around and leaned over onto the log that just happened to be at the correct height, she whimpered when he freed his cock from her hand. But his fingers sliding into her pussy made her forget everything but what he was doing to her. And Christ, the things he was doing to her made her weep tears of amazing feelings.

"I'm going to eat you, suck your pussy until you come in my mouth. Then I'm going to lap every bit of your cum in my mouth, making you come and come again." She cried out, wanting it now, not to wait on him. Pressing back, having him take her harder, she threw back her head and held onto the log tightly, digging her nails deeply into the hardwood.

"Please, Barron. Please." When he got down onto his knees and pulled her ass forward until her pussy was right on the edge of the log, she watched his head lower to her. "Barron, Please, I—"

His tongue entered her. She felt it move inside of her. In and out, in and out. When he licked her clit she threw back her head and lifted up her legs to go to him deeper. She wrapped her fingers in his hair and tried to guide him to her clit again, but he wouldn't.

When he finally took her clit into his mouth and sucked her hard, she screamed out her release. The birds and other animals flew off from the startling sound. And it made her smile. His fingers entered her, and again, he touched off another climax, then another. She lay back when he held his cock thick and hard before her.

"Watch me. Watch what I want to do when I come inside of you." His hand fisted his cock and stroked it once twice, then a third time before he came. Thick hot cum jettisoned out from him and onto her belly, breasts, and face. He roared with each release, and when he reached down and pinched her clit she came again, screaming out his name as he rubbed his cum all over her.

Willow couldn't move. She wasn't even sure she wanted to. Her mind and body were at peace for the first time in longer than she could remember. She opened one eye to look at Barron. He looked like he couldn't move either.

Barron was leaning against the tree heavily. His arms, down at his sides, were limp and covered in his cream. Turning his head ever so slightly so he could see her, his glazed eyes made her smile. He was just as turned inside out as she was. Maybe more so.

"We need a bath. Not only that, but a place to lie down and sleep for about an hour. I had no idea when…from now on, I'm going to invite you out here to relieve myself. I thought for sure that you'd be too sore to play around again.

"Never." Standing, she did need assistance in staying on her feet. With Barron holding onto her, she made her way to the same tree that he was leaning on and rested her head on his arm. Neither of them spoke for a while, which was wonderful. She didn't think she could concentrate on breathing and speaking at the same time.

"I'm going to see if I can get us home. Are you all right with me using a little magic? I don't know if it will work or not, but we need to get home soon before we spend the night out here in the cold." They were home in seconds. He didn't let go of her but took her to their bathroom to get some of the sweat and dirt off of them.

Then he reached into the shower stall and turned on the water. Steam rolled from the curtain as the bathroom heated up. When he stood up from the wall, she didn't know whether to be frightened or not when he came toward her. But he simply picked her up in his arms and pulled her into the shower.

"I think that I could sleep for a year. I'm so relaxed." He told her that he felt the same way and thought that if they were to go to bed right now, they'd wake up in the next century or somewhere long in the future."

They played around in the water, washing each other's bodies and kissing. Neither of them had enough energy to have sex again, but they did have fun. Once the hot water began to run out, they dried off and headed to the bed. She thought that she was asleep before the lights were out.

~*~

Ewing wasn't sure what was going on with his orchards, but he knew that someone was sabotaging the grapes. As he was walking around, trying to see how much damage had been done to the plants, he stopped when he saw what appeared to be a large family digging up some of his new starts. Watching them, he could hear that the man was a brut and was smacking around the kids like they were nothing but labor. Clearing his throat, the youngest of the children, about six, came running to him and hid behind him. That alone was enough to make him reach out to his brothers to let them know where he was and what was going on.

"Can I help you? This is private property you're on. I'm sure that you're aware of that, as there are signs all over the place. In fact, there are two of them right there where you're standing." The other child he didn't know the sex as they were bald, as if someone had taken an electric razor to their head and botched up their hair. It might well have been fresh, too, as there were bloodied places still bleeding in places. "Come here, please. I won't harm you." The child, he could see now that it was another little girl, ran toward him only to be tripped when the man backhanded her. "Come here, child. I won't hurt you."

Crawling on her belly, she made her way toward him only to be stomped on by the man. Going straight to the man, he used a bit of his bear to knock the man back, then picked up the child. She was sobbing, and he was sure that it had more to be in pain than her finally getting free of the man.

"You let go of my kids right now, or so help me, I'm going to kill you where you stand. They're mine." The child in his arms said that they weren't his kids and that he'd kidnapped them a few weeks ago. "You shut that trap of yours, kid, or so help me, you're going to regret you ever being born."

"I'm sure they do feel that way now." Amelia appeared and then disappeared with the children. What surprised him the most was the fact that the man didn't seem all that surprised by what had happened. He just stood there with his arms nearly over his massively fat chest and glared. "If you're trying to impress me, it's not working."

He didn't even look at his brothers as their bears as they came up behind the man. He didn't want to kill the man, not yet at any rate, but he did want answers. So he asked the man why he was on private property.

"You're right. It is private property, and it's mine. You should get your fancy little ass out of here before I get really mad and knock you on your ass." It was then that Mark growled. It was frightening, even to him, and he knew that they were related. The man turned around and fell on his ass while trying to get back away from the bears. It got close enough that Ewing was able to grab the man in a tight headlock and hold him still.

"You see those bears right there? They're my brothers and haven't had a good run to chase down their prey in a good long time. I'm going to let you go, and if you run, I surely hope that you've all your property, not this one, in order. They'll kill you where you stand." Mark took two steps toward the man and swiped him across the leg. Ewing was sure that all of them could smell the urine as the man had pissed himself. "Mark, now I'm going to have to go home and change again."

"Amelia didn't want to distract you, but she said to tell you that the girls aren't related and that she's taken them to the hospital. Both girls have been brutally beaten, and the older one has been abused with what she thinks was a whip. They've not said a word only to ask if you could come and protect them again." He told Mark to tell them that he'd be there as soon as he was finished with this man. *"All right. They won't let anyone touch them until you get there, so let's get this shithead taken care of and go there for them. If you back up, I'll make sure that he has a lesson in manners when it comes to people smaller than him."*

"All right. But don't kill him." He could actually feel Mark pouting. "Please don't kill him. We don't know what's going on right now, and I'd hate to find out that not only does he have these two children but more. Then you can kill him."

"Thanks." It was the strangest thing to see a big assed bear smile. It must have freaked the man out a little because he whimpered again. It was funny to him that this man had so much bravo when it was just him, and when nearly a half dozen bears showed up, he was as wimpy as a kitten. *"Amelia will come and get you. She'll take you directly to the hospital so you can see the kids. She also has a change of clothing for you."*

Grinning when Amelia suddenly appeared in front of him. He was in clean pants, and he smelled better, too. With just a touch to his arm, he was in a hospital room with the girls. As if he had known them for all their life, the two of them leapt from the hospital bed and wrapped their arms around him. Holding onto them while they sobbed, he got the information that he needed on the little girls.

"Their names are Rachel and Beth, I think it's just Beth. The younger has been with Ben Kinsley for the last several weeks. He beats her daily, and when that doesn't satisfy him, he locks her in an animal cage and lets his dogs, who he's trained to kill, try and get at her. The older one, Beth, knows Rachel, but only because they go to the same school. They didn't interact with each other there, but they've been clinging to each other since they were snatched. Rachel has been trying to teach the rules to Beth, but it doesn't seem to matter much. He still beats the two of them when he feels like they've done something wrong."

"Have you found their parents?" She said that all she could get out of their jumbled mind was that they'd been at school on the playground and suddenly woke up in the man's house. Same MO for both kidnappings. "Why did they trust me when they saw me coming up on them? Or is this just a case of them clinging to the first person that didn't reach out and knock the shit out of them? Either way, I'm thrilled to be able to save them."

"Kinsley has been killed." He hadn't expected that, but when she went on to explain, it made sense. "He leapt over the waterfall—why the hell do people do that when the chips are down, and he was killed almost instantly. As for clinging to you, you had it right on both scores. You didn't hit them, and you were kind to them. Kinsley has been trading them around to his buddies to beat up when they want some fun. Fuckers. I'm going to find out who they were and show them what it's like to have the shit beat out of you when you're smaller than someone else."

The doctor came in, and the girls held tightly to him. After asking him if they could have a female doctor, the children were frightened. The doctor seemed to understand completely and stepped out of the room. Before anyone else came in, Ewing reached into the minds of both girls one at a time to find out what else might be going on. Since he was touching them, it was easier for him to sort through their minds.

"Rachel's mother died when she was twenty-two of an overdose. One of her relatives sold her to Kinsley. Poor kid had been bounced from family to family. She's had a rough life. Beth's parents are looking for her, but not in a good way. They've never been paid by Kinsley when she was sold to him, as well. Both are in one of the abandoned hotels along the strip, too. They've been looking for other kids to snatch, and — I have to ask this. Why the fuck do people have children if they're going

to just abuse and hurt them? I mean, get a fucking job and work like the rest of us have to do." Amelia asked him if he was all right just as the female doctor walked into the room. *"No, I'm not all right. These kids are happier with me, a complete stranger, than they are with their own parents. There has to be something someone can do to fix this, don't you think?"*

"Christ, I don't know." The doctor told the girls that they were very brave that they'd found Ewing when they did. The kids never spoke to the doctor, but they watched every move she made. As soon as they were asked to put on the gowns so that they could go to get some x-rays, Ewing wanted to go and find their parents and kill them. Even the ones that were dead? He thought that they'd gotten off too easily.

"Honey, can you tell me who burnt you? And if you've been hurt like this before?" The doctor was trying her best to keep her cool, and he was impressed with her. Again, neither child spoke, but they clung to him still. "How do you know these children, Mr. Cross?"

"I come upon them when they were with another person who was beating them. I didn't do this." She told him that she didn't think that he had. "Thank you for that. However, if it helps, the man who did do it is dead. I didn't do that either, though, I wish I had."

When they were taken to x-ray, he had to go with them. While one was being photographed, the other sat on his lap and held onto his hand. Then, they traded places when it was the other's turn. They didn't scream or cry when the doctor checked their many and bad wounds, but they did look at him when someone new they came in contact with them. As soon as they were put in a room on the nursery floor, both girls got into one of the beds in the room, holding each other and his hands, and went to sleep. Of course, it helped, he supposed, that they were given something for pain that helped a great deal.

The police showed up about an hour later. The bodies had been found, and the other two had been arrested. When asked if he'd step outside, he told the officer that if they woke and he was gone, he didn't know if they'd calm down again or not. So, the two of them spoke quietly so as not to disturb the children.

"There were four more children in the house where the couple were. They'll be brought in as soon as the scene is cleared. Christ, Ewing, I don't think I've ever seen a bigger mess than the one those children were living in. The couple, not married, are here under lock and key and have no idea that the children have been found. I'd like to keep it that way for a while." Ewing said that he understood. "Thanks. Also, you should know that we still don't know any last names or last known addresses. Since the place they were staying has been empty for some time now, there isn't anything to indicate who they might have been."

"Are you asking for my help?" He nodded and grinned. "Beth's last name is Carter. She has four siblings. I don't know where they are as she doesn't know. Rachel's mother is Howard. She has been in and out of jail a great deal since she turned eighteen. She was only twenty-two when she killed herself with the coke. Rachel has been bouncing from relative to relative until she met up with this last one and sold her to Kinsley. There are three more children out there that belong to her. I believe that it was Kinsley that sold them off. But I can't be sure about that right now." The officer asked him the same thing that he'd asked Amelia. "I can't answer that. I truly wish that I could, but

I don't know. People, humans suck, don't you think?"

"Since I'm a human, I'm not going to answer that for you." He laughed, not much, but it did relieve some of the tension in his head. "With these names, I'll be able to chase down someone to see about taking the kids. Can I depend on your family to keep them safe until then? I was told that no one can touch them unless you're in the room with them. Is that true?"

"I don't know why, but yeah, that's true. What are people going to say if they find out an unrelated male is taking care of two little girls." He told him that it was six children. "No. I was there, there were—Pete, I don't know if I can handle six kids? I can barely remember to get my laundry out of the washer before it goes sour, and I have to rewash everything. How old are these kids anyway?"

One is an infant. But to be honest with you, Ewing, I don't think that he's going to make it without some help in the way you can do it. The others look to be anywhere from two to ten. Just little buggers that will be in the system if you don't do this." He called him a few choice names, then said he'd take them. "I was hoping you'd say that. I think that your sisters have already adopted them into the family."

"Great. Now, if I have a mate out there, she's going to be running to town because I've already got too many kids for two people to handle." Pete laughed. "All right. They can stay with me. But I'm also going to need some help with them. Where is the little boy now? The infant?"

They brought him in a few minutes later. He was a tiny little thing, and even with all the machines hooked up to him, Ewing knew that he more than likely wasn't going to make it. Reaching down to take him out of the little crib, careful of the wires, he pulled him close to him and had the officer slice a hole in his hand.

"He's not taking it. If he doesn't, Pete, I'll call my—he is taking it in now." When Pete left him, he was told by the nurses that they didn't have a name for the baby. But they thought that he'd been released as soon as a few days ago from being born. They thought his name was Williams, who was the most recently released baby that would have been about the time frame of his age.

The girls slept through the night, again

thanks to the meds they'd been given. Every once in a while, one of the nurses would come for Billy, what he decided to call the little man, and change and weigh him. Every time he was brought back to him, it seemed to be about every four hours, he'd give him a bit more of his blood to help him out. He didn't know what he'd do if the little guy went to another family. His hold over him would be great if he kept feeding him to live.

Ewing thought to himself that, at this point, he didn't care. When he could, he walked to the room next door to check on the three children there. They were all girls but for the infant, and he couldn't help but kiss them on their forehead while they were resting. Just as the sun was coming up, realizing how he'd not slept a wink, his family joined him to help spread out being with the kids. Also, they had brought him some much-needed food.

Between rooms, he was learning a great deal about the family. The three children, not counting Billy, were six, seven, and eight years old. Their names a little fuzzy on that since most of the time they'd been called hateful names instead of their names, so he decided to call them, by oldest to youngest, Harper, Lily, and Patty. When they woke up, he'd call them what they wanted but it helped him be able to keep the six of them straight while talking to his family and the staff about them. Christ, he wished more than ever that his grannie was around. She'd be getting such a kick out of all these kids around. She'd also have a bit of advice for him on how to care for them.

Coming back from the bathroom, he noticed that Beth was talking to Patty. As soon as he sat down to get comfy, Patty asked if he would adopt her too. It took him a few minutes to realize that these kids expected him to raise them as his own.

"I don't know where your parents are. Do you?" Patty shook her head and said she'd not seen them in weeks. "You'll be staying with me and the rest of my family if the police allow it. I'm a single man and don't know a great deal about children, but we'll get through it."

By evening, little Joey was taking his bottle well and looking better all the time. He was a cute little guy and, like all the other children, had a head full of curly blond hair. Amelia used some of her magic to give Rachel some semblance of hair, and it made them all happy. By the time that lunch rolled around for them, Ewing needed a break just to get out of the hospital. The smells were getting to him, and he didn't want to sit around for too long before he started getting sore.

He was surprised when the doctor from the emergency department joined him. He asked her if she was doing all right, and after telling him that she was finished with a double shift, she asked him why he'd take on so many kids.

"My grandparents. They really were my grandparents. Unlike these kids who have no idea who they belong to, my grandparents took us all into their homes and raised all six of us. It had to be hard on them, they were already in their mid to late seventies by then, and six rambunctious boys couldn't have been easy. I promised my grannie that when I was older, I would do what she did and not leave anyone, children especially left alone if I could do anything about it. I have the means, the house as well as love enough to go around. Besides, I'm thinking that some of these children will find their own parents, and I'll just have a couple. Not that it matters, really. I'd love to have a houseful of kids."

"You aren't married." He smiled and shook

his head. "You're a bear. I'm to understand, too. Wealthy and smart. Yet I don't think you're doing this for any other reason than you want to. Not to show off to some woman."

"No, I don't believe that if the right woman came along, she'd care about how many children I'm raising. She'd just be happy that I'm not going to have to work thirty jobs to put them through college when the time comes. So that I can be there to change diapers and make dinner." She asked if he could do either of those. "I can, as a matter of fact. Changing the diaper isn't something that I'd say I was a pro at, but I do get the right parts covered up. I have to read the box once to remember how to put a diaper on right, but like I said, I get there. Are you looking for the job?"

He knew she wasn't his mate, but she did tell him that she had enough going on without adding a bunch of kids to the mix. After telling her how he'd come upon the first two little girls, it was like a sudden spring thaw when he suddenly had six kids. Standing up when he felt the children waking up, he told her that it was nice meeting her.

"Pauline Dixion." He didn't know what she

meant. "I'm married, happily so, but that's my name. Pauline Dixon. Call me if you need advice or help. I'm one of eleven children in my family."

Ewing was still laughing as he made his way into the hospital again. As soon as he walked into the room, all five of the kids tried to get onto his lap. As soon as the last one was settled, or as settled as he could be with five beautiful little girls surrounding him, he closed his eyes. Just a small nap, he told himself. He realized that he was going to need to do this more often, take a nap when he could, or he'd never get any sleep. Smiling, he let sleep take him under.

Before You Go...

HELP AN AUTHOR

write a review

THANK YOU!

Share your voice and help guide other readers to these wonderful books. Even if it's only a line or two, your reviews help readers discover the author's books so they can continue creating stories that you'll love. Log in to your favorite retailer and leave a review. Thank you.

Kathi Barton, a winner of the Pinnacle Book Achievement Award and a best-selling author on Amazon and All Romance books, lives in Nashport, Ohio, with her husband, Paul. When not creating new worlds and romance, Kathi and her husband enjoy camping and going to auctions. She can also be seen at county fairs with her husband, an artist and potter.

Her muse, a cross between Jimmy Stewart and Hugh Jackman, brings her stories to life for her readers in a way that has them coming back time and again for more. Her favorite genre is paranormal romance, with a great deal of spice. You can visit Kathi online and drop her an email if you'd like. She loves hearing from her fans. aaronskiss@gmail.com.

Follow Kathi on her blog: http://kathisbartonauthor.blogspot.com/